RADGEPACKET

Tales from the Inner Cities

Volume Two

A collection of short fiction from around Great Britain.

Featuring

Danny King
Ian Ayris
Darrell Irving
Dorothy Crossan
Melissa Mann
Joe Ridgwell
Roz Southey

Will Diamond
Fiona Glass
Martin Reed
Lorna Windham
Patrick Belshaw
Craig Douglas
S A Tranter

and introducing

Sheila Quigley

Published by:-

Byker Books
66 Kings Road
Banbury
Oxon
OX16 0DJ

www.bykerbooks.co.uk

2008

ISBN 978-0-9560788-1-0

YUP WE'RE BACK...

It turns out you all liked Volume One so much that we thought we'd better bring out a second collection sharpish if only to make the threatening letters cease.

We've welcomed back some old friends in this issue and have acquired some new authors who we're sure you'll enjoy.

We've got stories about hard men in soft shirts, squaddie shenanigans, chavs up mountains, the North/South divide, tarts with hearts, ageing rock stars and ooh...loads more.

The mighty Danny King has left another exclusive story lying around again and we've snaffled it when his back was turned - that'll learn him.

On top of all this, we've even managed to snag an interview with well known crime fiction author Sheila Quigley as well as an exclusive story and some of her books to give you in another free competition.

If you read the first issue then you'll know that some of this stuff isn't for the eyes of those who may be offended by 'adult' or near the knuckle material. If on the other hand you like that kind of thing then read on....you're gonna love it.

Happy reading.

Ed

SO LET'S CRACK ON...

Contents

My Gay Shirt	Will Diamond	5
Breaking Point	Lorna Windham	13
The Gay Downstairs	S A Tranter	25
Trick	Melissa Mann	31
Trains	Ian Ayris	35
The Law of the Jungle	Darrell Irving	38
The Likely Lads	Craig Douglas	49
The Crossing	Patrick Belshaw	70
Rock and a Hard Place	Fiona Glass	80
Sheena up a Mountain Wearing Flip Flops	Martin Reed	91
The Underpass	Dorothy Crossan	102
Portrait of the Artist as a Young Man.	Joe Ridgwell	112
The Sleep Walker	Danny King	122
Another Life	Roz Southey	130

Extras

Featuring Sheila Quigley

The Radgepacket Tapes	143
Black Betty	148
Win signed copies of Sheila's books	155

<u>Will Diamond</u>

William Diamond exists in every mind in the country. He is brash, loveable, untrustworthy and a bit of a pain in the arse to be honest. He is your worst neighbour and your best mate. He likes all things wrong and excels at breaking the rules. But hey, he's a Gateshead lad so who fucking cares.

My Gay Shirt

My face must have been a picture when I tore open the wrapping paper. I mean yeah, I like my designer labels. But a 'Silver' Armani shirt was just a little bit more than I was expecting.

'Do you like it?' questioned both Deb and her mother.

It really scared me when they spoke in unison; it was like looking into the future, and believe me it wasn't looking too good.

'It's...yeah...well it's fine.'

'Ooh he doesn't like it,' says the mother-in-law in that tone only she can use.

'No...I do like it...honest.'

She flashes a brown-toothed grin at Deb and everyone apart from me is happy. So that was the start of a very bad fortieth birthday.

*****

I spent most of the day on the phone, organising that night's events. I could see Deb was getting annoyed at hearing the route of my intended pub-crawl over and over again but I also knew she had the added satisfaction of knowing that I would be sporting the new shirt her mother had purchased.

I finished up my phone call and headed up the wooden hill that is the stairs. The shower was raining down on me as I popped the top on the old 'Head and Shoulders' and gave what was left of my hair a good scrubbing. It was out with the Davidoff body wash with particular attention given to mini me and his dangling twin brothers. Then I went through the normal shaving routine and moved on to the bedroom.

Black Calvin boxers, black socks with a little St. George's cross on them, nice pair of Replay jeans-slightly stonewashed-then my hideous silver Armani shirt. Topped off with a nice pair of casual Lacoste shoes. I looked in the mirror and one word sprung to mind...Poofta!

You see women don't understand. They chase fashion, but men just fall into it. Sure you experiment when you're young but then you find something comfortable and that's you sorted. I've been a jeans and shirt man for the last twenty years, well barring the old suit for weddings, christenings, funerals and boxing nights.

*****

'You look lovely pet.'

Yeah she would say that, knowing there's more chance of me meeting 'Chase me Charlie I'm made of fucking chocolate' than a Cheryl Cole look-a-like. How the fuck did Ashley manage to bag that beauty anyway?

'There's the taxi love,' I gave her a quick peck and I was heading out the door.

'Will,' I looked back towards the door, 'be careful.'

I nodded and jumped into the waiting car.

'Will be careful,' cried all the lads as we pulled away. And the car erupted into laughter. Wankers.

Being the last one in the car I was sitting in the front and getting hit for the 'tenner' fare over to Newcastle. The lads were cracking on as usual in the back of the cab, when I noticed the taxi driver giving me a sly eye. I waited to see if he would look again and he did.

'Fuck you looking at, eh?'

The taxi driver just burst out laughing and said 'nice shirt mate.'

The lads, who hadn't really noticed my shirt, had now all taken an interest in the silver item.

'What the fuck you got on Will?' Asked Dave.

'Right that's it, stop the fucking cab now. I'm fucking warning you mate, pull the fuck over now.'

The taxi driver pulled in to the side of the road as I pulled the door open. The cunt didn't think it was funny now as I yanked open his door and dragged the fucker screaming from the car. He got a swift one in the face that dropped him to the floor where his head had an argument with my Lacoste slip-ons. His head lost out badly before the lads could drag me away.

'What the fuck you thinking of Will?' Screamed Dave, as Joe and Alan looked on.

'That cunt said my shirt was a faggot's shirt, fucking tosser.'

Dave shook his head as the four of us walked away and headed towards Newcastle on foot. Not before I had slipped over to where the taxi driver lay and informed him that if the Police got wind of what had happened, he'd get twice the beating the next time. And so my birthday began.

*****

First stop was the Centurion bar. A bit pricey but a nice pub all the same and let's face it I wasn't buying so who fucking cares? Dave ordered the drinks, mine being a Lager with a Flat-Liner chaser. Flat-Liners for anyone that doesn't know is a shot of Sambuca, a shot of Tequila and a few drops of Tabasco sauce that make a red line separating the two alcohols. Fucking dangerous, but nice all the same.

We got talking to a couple of fat, fish gutters from over Byker way. They were well up for it but we weren't to be honest. Not enough alcohol, their loss not ours like. Let's face it; you take your life in your hands shagging someone's daughter from Byker anyway. So we moved over to where the door that leads to the Central Station was. Hoping to spot some nice fresh fanny getting off one of the trains. The train from Darlington pulled in.

'Look sharp lads,' Dave said. 'You know them Darlo lasses like the cock and they all swallow the fat as well.'

Unfortunately for us the only twats to get off the train were a group of blokes who looked like they were on a stag night. They headed over to where we were stood and walked into the bar. A few nods and winks and 'alrights' and they were past us and up to the counter screaming for drinks. We settled down to some football banter. With the odd Cheryl Cole lust story thrown in. Lucky bastard that Ashley, did I mention that before.

Anyway, things were going okay until I decided to go the toilet. I've walked in and unleashed the Python in the general direction of the piss trough, when some cunt behind me in a slow droning Darlo accent says 'Oooooh honey I like your shirt.'

I just stared straight ahead at the ever-thinning line of piss coming from mini-me. A quick shake and back he went into my trousers. The fucker didn't even see it coming. The first he knew about it was when he felt my Neanderthal brow make contact with his nose cartilage. The poor bastard had no luck as he fell backwards through the toilet cubicle and got wedged down between the wall and the pot.

I personally thought it would have taken a couple to down him but I was wrong. He was out cold, but on a brighter note, his mate who was now cowering in the corner would be able to help him up. I went back into the bar and suggested we move on.

*****

We ended up doing the usual pub-crawl around the quayside before we headed on to a club. The queue wasn't too bad; there were only about twenty people in front of us. Most of them were lasses so things were looking up. As I reached the front of the queue the doorman put his hand out and stopped me.

'Sorry mate you can't get in,'

'What for?' I asked. 'I've had a few but I'm okay.'

'Sorry mate, I can't let you in.'

'For fucks sake mate, it's my fortieth birthday and I've had a few pints with the lads. Don't go fucking spoiling it for me.'

'Look, whether it's your birthday or not I can't let you in.'

'Why?'

'I don't need to give you a reason.'

'Yes you fucking do. Get me the manager if you can't give me a reason. Maybe he'll let me in.'

'Look mate, I don't need a reason and I'm not getting the

manager so fuck off.'

'Fuck you, I'm not moving until you tell me why I can't come in.'

'Right then, lets just say it's because your shirt makes you look like a poof.'

The doorman burst out laughing and so did his mate. They were looking at me as though I was some sort of mug. I glanced at the lads who were looking a bit worried, then I spun around and planted a fucking wind-milled right hand right on the bastards temple. The fat fucka hit the floor like a bag of wet shit. The lads dragged the other doorman out into the open where we gave him a right good fucking kicking.

We eventually took to our heels and headed off into the night. The lads wanted to go on to another club but I'd had enough. I said my goodbyes and headed back up to the Central Station to get a taxi home.

The queue was fucking massive when I got there so I lit a fag and waited patiently. In all fairness it was going down quite quickly, so I lit another fag and started to hum a song in my head. There was a car pulling in for two girls in front of me then I was next. As it pulled in two blokes behind me tried to jump the queue.

'Whoa lads,' I shouted, 'These two ladies are first then it's me.'

'Alright mate, keep your fucking hair on.'

'I'm just saying lads, c'mon lets not spoil a good night out.'

'I know mate, I'm only winding you up.'

I winked at one of the lads to sort of show everything was

okay and turned back to look at the girls.

'Thanks for that,' one of the girls said as she got in the car.

'No bother,' I returned.

As the car pulled away I turned to look at the two lads who had jumped the queue. In all fairness I was about to get my tabs out and offer them one. The taller one of the two was laughing as he looked at me and said...

'Nice shirt mate...'

<u>Lorna Windham</u>

Lorna was the winner of the 'North Tyneside Short Story Contest' and longlisted in the Times 'Chicken House Childrens Novel' Competition in 2008. She lives with a delinquent cat, a very patient husband and a host of imaginary characters with seemingly insoluble problems.

<u>The Breaking Point</u>

Stuart couldn't find the note. Why? Liz was always tidying up. He'd left it on the sofa and she'd said it was by the phone. Well, he'd looked in both places and it wasn't there.

'Write down the arrangements again,' she'd said. She was his eldest daughter and always fussing.

'I know when my birthday is.'

'But it's the time and the place, Dad. You know how bad your memory is these days.' Well, no he didn't actually.

Then she said they'd agreed she'd pick him up, 'they' being his son Tim and daughter Hattie.

'I'll make it under my own steam thanks.'

Liz seemed a bit put out. So was he. She'd told everyone he was incapable of making journeys on his own.He and Kay had supported their children for years, but the kids had flown the nest and returned so many times you'd think they were carrier pigeons. They'd shaken their heads over their children all their lives.

Stuart had been a widower for five years and now he was sure heads were being shaken over him. He didn't like it, in fact he resented it. He'd show them. But where the hell was that note? A frustrating hour later he found it under an album by the phone. Liz was right. How bloody annoying. He booked a ticket from Jarrow to Alnmouth Station. He'd change trains at Newcastle and get a taxi to the 'White Swan Hotel' in Alnwick. After all he was only seventy eight once.

Pushing the album out of the way it fell on the floor. A fad-ing yellowing photograph stared at him. The memories flood-ed back. He was a fair, freckle faced youth back then. Barely fifteen, he wore a new Post Office uniform, one of only two messenger boys, leaning on a mail van.

It was his first job in a town that had eighty percent unemployment. He'd been lucky, very lucky. One of his mam's cousins worked in the Post Office and told her a job was going for a young lad and he'd got it and meant to keep it. He'd seen enough of the groups of lean men in threadbare suits, flat caps and white mufflers standing on street corners. There was little work in Jarrow then and you could see it in men's eyes.

Now where was he going tomorrow? Thirty minutes later he'd located the damned note again. It had mysteriously moved to the sofa. Tired out he went to bed.

The next day dawned bright and early. There was something special about it. What was it? Getting out of bed he stood on his spectacles. Damn.

Nursing a slightly bruised foot, he limped into the kitchen and peered through crooked, gold frames at the date Liz had ringed on the calendar. It was his seventy eighth birthday. Memories of his parents and two brothers, long gone now, came and went like the tide. There was only him and his children left now. He wiped his eyes. No point in feeling maudlin, he had a journey to make.

All his travel arrangements worked like clockwork. At exactly one o'clock he found himself in Alnwick, outside the 'White Swan'. Feeling extremely pleased he pushed his way through the revolving door and enjoyed the fresh aroma of polish and wood. The hotel had recently been tastefully refurbished in creams and earth colours and a carved wooden fireplace dominated the room. Comfortable leather arm chairs beckoned on the left. He sat in one and waited for everyone to arrive.

High up, in a recess, the model of a ship with a black hull, white decks, two masts and four white funnels looked down on him. Something stirred in his cobweb memory, dusted itself off and waited. The past and the present met. There he was again, a messenger boy with Mr. Hodge the clerk looking over his spectacles at him wheezing, 'I've got a telegram for you lad.' His ruined voice a constant reminder he'd survived a gas attack in the First World War.

'You're to take it to that ship at Palmers Yard. The recipient's on here.'

He thrust a crisp orange envelope into Stuart's hand and wagged a bony finger at him, 'and no mucking about mind. I'll expect you back inside the hour. There's plenty out there would like your job and you'd do well to remember that.'

There was no need to ask which ship. She had brought much needed work. The piers at Tynemouth and South Shields had been full of people dressed in their best clothes, cheering loudly and waving when she'd steamed up the Tyne, surrounded by tugs and other craft, a few days before. A brass band had played all the old tunes like 'Pack up your troubles in your old kit bag', 'Goodbye Dolly Gray' and 'Rule Britannia'. Children waved their red, blue and white flags and hats were thrown in the air in recognition of who she was; what she'd done and the work she'd bring.

Stuart whizzed down towards the Tyne with all the energy of a fifteen year old, the wind whistling past his ears, coat flying and the telegram safely tucked in his leather pouch. He pretended he was a pony express rider being chased by red indians. His mam blamed too many nights at the flicks; Dad just blamed him.

He arrived at Palmers Yard and waited for the gatekeeper, Mr. Mulligan, to finish his conversation with a group of shabbily dressed men looking for jobs.

'Come back tomorrow,' he was saying, 'we might be taking a few lads on then.' They left with heads and shoulders bowed, unwilling victims of the depression. Behind him the air was filled with the dull banging and clanking of those at work. He wiped his walrus moustache with a meaty hand and raised a bushy eyebrow in query, 'Yes?'

'Telegram for Captain Vaughan,' Stuart showed him the orange envelope.

A hand on his shoulder brought him back to the present with a jolt.

'Excuse me sir, are you Mr. Wilson, Mr. Stuart Wilson?'

'Yes that's me.'

'I've a message.'

'Thanks.' He opened it, read it and put it in his pocket. Unable to resist he turned back to the ship and the past rushed forward to meet him once again.

'The ship's down at the quay, you can't miss her,' said Mr. Mulligan with a jerk of his bull head in the direction he should go.

'We're gutting her, ready for auction before she's dismantled.'

He was right. The sheer scale of her was overwhelming and the noise became an un-orchestrated cacophony as Stuart advanced to meet her. He could make out the individual sounds of nails being carefully pulled from their resting places; the hissing of acetylene torches and the harsh cutting of metal. Burning, dusty, rusty smells invaded his nostrils and caught at the back of his throat.

She lay next to the ferry landing. Given the working name of

'Star No.400' by Harland and Wolff and launched in Belfast in Nineteen Eleven she was meant for the lucrative trans-Atlantic trade along with her sister ships. Now she had men swarming all over her like worker ants taking her apart bit by bit. The black and white gulls wisely stayed on the river's edge well away from the echoing and reverberating sounds.

The local newspapers had been full of how she had five full decks and a steel hull. How as a pleasure passenger liner she had the capacity to take over two thousand passengers, unheard of when she was launched. Her war record had earned her the nickname 'Old Reliable' because as a troop-ship she'd carried hundreds of thousands of troops from Liverpool to Gallipoli; from Halifax, Nova Scotia and America to Britain. She was most famous for being the only warship in WWI to have rammed a German U-boat and sunk it!

How Stuart wished he'd sailed on her, been to the places she'd been and shared in her adventures.

He'd thought she was big when she'd passed between the piers, but up close she was massive like a grand old lady dressed up with nowhere to go. He climbed the gangway, excitement mounting, as he explored her white decks.

His family lived in a downstairs flat in Bede Street. It was one of several grey industrial terraces. There was no money for luxuries. In contrast, this ship in her day was the ultimate in luxury and he was eager to see how the other half lived. He'd read about the Duke of this and the Duchess of that, but had no idea of the sort of lifestyle their wealth bought them. He was dying to find out.

A whiff of diesel and oil fumes wafted up from the engine room as a series of workmen and members of the skeleton crew pointed Stuart along a maze of corridors to where the captain was.

'He's in the first class lounge, up those stairs and through the door,' said one gesturing behind him with a dirty thumb.

Stuart entered the sanctuary of the lounge. It was another world. The best materials and craftsmen had been used and it showed. A white, ornately decorated ceiling had tear drop chandeliers suspended from it; woodwork was a gilded forest of intricately carved fruit and leaves and twinkling glass had oval amber motifs of beautiful women in classical dress playing musical instruments.

'Take a long look, son,' said Captain Vaughan coming towards Stuart, 'you'll never see this room again.'

'Happy birthday Dad,' said Liz bringing him back to the present with a quick peck on the cheek. 'Is there something wrong with your specs? Journey alright? I'd have come to pick you up you know. It wouldn't have been any bother.'

'What?'

'You day dreaming again?' Hattie gave him a hug, 'happy birthday. Your specs look a bit...'

'I know.'

Tim shook his hand, 'Your specs are crooked. Let me.' They were ripped off Stuart's face, expertly mangled in huge paws and replaced. Tim looked at him from all angles and then gave his usual wry grin.

'You might have to buy a new pair; happy birthday anyway. Let me buy you all a pre-dinner drink. Now what'll it be?'

'Just a lager for me thanks,' Stuart snapped. Tim never had been practical. They all raised their eyebrows as Stuart sat glowering behind ruined spectacles in a wing chair by the fire. The girls twittered away as he opened his presents: slippers from Liz; a dressing gown from Hattie and pyjamas from Tim. Stuart downed the lager in one. He needed it. What were his offspring trying to tell him?

The dinner gong sounded and they headed for the dining room.

'Come on dad,' urged Tim who was standing at the top of some intricately carved light oak stairs, 'the girls are waiting.'

The meal was pleasant and the surroundings glorious. They'd finished the coffee and mints and Stuart was deep in thought about the past. When you're young you live for the moment, you don't give much thought to a great ship being broken up; her heart ripped out and her insides on display for every Tom, Dick or Harry to bid for. There was something slightly distasteful about the auction, shameful even. Stuart had heard of one man buying a door from that wonderful ship and putting it on his pigeon cree.

Liz's voice brought him back to the present with a bump.

'Dad we've been talking. You know we all love and worry about you now that mam's gone. We'd liked you to have stayed with one of us, but our houses are just not suitable. You're not getting any younger...'   She looked at the others for help.

'We thought you might want to think about moving into more secure accommodation,' added Hattie trying to be help-ful.

'If you look at the brochure...' Tim's voice trailed away.

'What would I want to do that for?' Stuart said gruffly.   It was hard to keep the resentment out of his voice. 'I've an announcement to make. As you all appear to feel I'm not fit to sail under my own steam anymore...'

'Oh come on Dad,' protested Tim.

'No, hear me out. I've decided my best days are ahead of me.
I've worked since I was fifteen years old and I never knew
what luxury was till I set foot in the first class lounge of the
'Olympic' when I was a lad. She was the 'Titanic's' sister ship
by the way.'

'The Titanic...and you were in the 'Olympic's lounge?' They
looked at him in astonishment.

'I was delivering a telegram to the captain before she was
broken up and auctioned off. You see that oak panelling; the
ceiling; the mantelpiece; the glass; not to mention the stairs
we came up? They're from the first class lounge on the
'Olympic.'

'What?'

'It was a sad end to a great ship, but at least some part of her
has been preserved for future generations to enjoy. The last
time I saw this room was over sixty years ago and now I've
eaten a meal in it surrounded, I'm sure, by well heeled ghosts
from the past. It's a funny old world.'

'I never knew,' said Liz.

'You never asked. You know your mother and I weren't well
off as I worked my way up in the Post Office. We scrimped
and saved all our lives. Whenever an insurance policy paid
out we spent it on you. Well, I'm seventy eight and I'm going
to do what I want for a change.'

'But Dad...' began Liz.

'No let me have my say. I promised myself something that
day on the 'Olympic' and this is it. If I ever had the opportunity to sail on a ship like that I'd take it.'

Liz wasn't listening, she was looking behind his shoulder at a startlingly dressed woman who was all sparkling earrings; bleached hair and red high heels.

'Stu, darling you got my message I hope.' She kissed him on both cheeks much to everyone's consternation.

'I did.'

She cocked her head at a strange angle and said, 'Your specs...'

'I know. Sorry you couldn't make the meal. Meet the family. This is Sheila everyone, a good... friend. Sheila these are my children Liz, Hattie and Tim.'

There was a stunned silence, followed by a slow rush of icy hellos.

'Take a seat Sheila. Get her a coffee someone.' She sat down beside him.

'You may as well know that Sheila and I are going to share a luxury cabin with a balcony while we cruise round the Med. And before you ask, we've no intention of getting wed. I had enough of that with your mother.'

There was a slight tugging at his sleeve. He ignored it as he was bathing in the glow of his generosity.

'Good on you Dad and you too Sheila,' said Tim winking and raising his cup to them.

'Tim' snarled Liz, 'grow up.' It was then Stuart remembered why Liz's first husband had walked out on her and she'd left the second. Now she was looking for the third, God help him. Tim ignored her.

'By the time you get back I should have the new business underway.'

Tim, thank God, was unmarried but with two failed business ventures behind him. He hadn't listened to advice and hadn't let anyone know things were going wrong until it was too late. Did Stuart really want his son's endorsement?

'And Liz and I will probably have new men in our lives,' giggled Hattie as Liz glared at her.

Hattie, the one- time loose living hippie had travelled the world, and had numerous partners. She lived her life believing that fate would steer her course. Had she learned anything?

'Perhaps we could make it a world cruise?' Stuart mused oblivious of the tugging which had become frantic by now.

'Well, I'm shocked,' said Liz with the aggrieved air of a spoilt child, 'really Dad.'

Feeling that the stitching in his best Harris tweed was about to be ripped apart Stuart gave his full attention to Sheila,

'Mmm?'

'Now Stu, you didn't ask me did you? I don't do cruises; too much sea heaving up and down, enough to make you sick. What do you think Tim?'

She stared deeply into his eyes and flicked her hair a lot Stuart wasn't a cruel man, but it was now he realised Sheila and a praying mantis had a lot in common. Tim leered back at her.

'Bloody typical,' thought Stuart. Then came his master-stroke, 'I'll go on my own.'

'You can't just go off, not at your age, be reasonable you're...' started Liz.

'Seventy eight,' Stuart finished for her, 'and when were you lot ever reasonable? I'm not ready for the breaker's yard, not by a long chalk.'

He whipped off his spectacles to impress them with how serious he was. This was his downfall - the stem of one half remained in his right hand, whilst the other sailed in broken abandon into Sheila's coffee.

The ensuing laughter broke the silence and the ice, but not his spirit of adventure.

The cruise was on.

S A Tranter

S A Tranter lives in Edinburgh and has had stories published in print magazines in the UK and the US. He's had too many jobs, all of which he hated, but the night shift taxi driver paid the most.

The Gay Downstairs

I was hiding in the worst bars, running three hundred hangovers a year. Wine and ale mixed in the same pint glass with forty Marlboro red thrown in. It almost killed me. HIV was on the scene and everyone in these bars in those days hated the gays. Edinburgh was the AIDS capital of Europe. That was mostly due to the junkies. But the junkies and almost everyone else were blaming the gays.

There was one in the flat below me. I'd pass him on the stairwell, drunk and roaring with laughter I'd corner him and squeeze his bum cheeks and he loved it -I've nothing against the gays or the female for that matter - though the female does seem to have quite a lot against me. And he'd invite me in. He had three thousand books in there and he'd say:

'Take what you want Trants.'

And I think he was referring to the books. So I had a look but I'd read them all. Except Celine's: Journey to the End of the Night and Death on the Installment Plan. So I thank him for that. And Celine was good; almost the best. But he'd gone nazi in the end but so had Knut Hamsun.

The gay was a writer. I was trying to do something similar, and failing. But somehow that seemed okay. Maybe I lacked conviction, it was a shot in the dark and you needed much luck. My time would come. Or wouldn't. It didn't really matter.

'Read this,' he'd say, tossing me his latest work; a short story or poetry or the novel thing...the gay was good alright. He had style. Writing style. Style is the most important thing. After endurance it's the most important thing.

The gay knew a lot of folk; other writers. Publishers of small magazines and some not so small. He knew things about them.

'This one said he'd publish six of my poems if I sucked his dick.'

I knew he wanted me to ask; 'And did you Crispin'. So I kept quiet. Funny. He looked at me, his lips pursed. He kept looking. Bug eyes and pursed lips. It really was funny. Then: 'This one's married and lectures at Edinburgh University and is banging a seventeen year old student. He always bangs the youngest students.'

'Male or female?'

'Female...the sluts.'

We'd play chess and pass the poppers bottle. He beat me every time. I think in the end he did make it as a novelist or formed a band or opened his wrists in a bathtub. Something.

'This one was fucking that one's wife in the arse. And the husband found out and went berserk cos his wife had never let him fuck her in the arse.'

'I can see his point, what happened, what did the husband do?'

'He used his fists. On his wife. The two men are still pals though, and they're both very good writers, the husband and the arse shagger.'

'Ah well then.'

# # #

Then I had some trouble. I'd go for a piss immediately after shagging or wanking - or have a wank or a shag immediately after pissing, I forget the order - and my cock burned and

drip dripped all night. I was mad with booze and the piss
cock pain and ran naked round the flat turning the taps on
and off. I stood over the cats litter tray feet either side.
Standing there I drank wine from the bottle. My cock hanging down, dangling and drip dripping the cloudy piss into the
cat litter.

I'd been so often to the Edinburgh clinic that they knew me
by sight and name and even a drunk can feel ashamed. So I
went to Glasgow and walked in. In the waiting room was an
old pal from AA whom I'd seen at the Edinburgh clinic a half
dozen times. Had shame trapped him too? Shame, fear and
embarrassment are the great driving forces.

'Awright Kenny,' I nodded.

'No bad Trants, yirsel?' he grinned.

Then they called me and I walked over and Kenny gave me
the thumbs up. It was a female nurse and I kept staring. God
if I could only get a woman like that. She told me to unzip
and pull them down. Luckily I'd put clean ones on that morning.

'What seems to be the problem Mr Tranter?'

But I was still staring. Hair, neck, breasts, legs. Back up to
the mouth.

'MR TRANTER.'

'Pardon?...oh yes, um, it stings when I pee. And it feels like I
have to pee all the time. But only dribbles come out.'

When she touched the thing it began to rise. She looked
alarmed then tapped it hard with a pencil. It did the trick.
The bitch. She was going for the old umbrella routine.
You know, the device that looks like a cocktail umbrella...no

pun intended. Some laugh.

She put the gloves on. She bent down almost to her knees in front of me. She was very close to me. She gripped my dick. And I smirked. Then she looked up at me and waved the umbrella thing. Shit. She had the power. But I knew what was coming and closed my eyes, did the breathing thing and tried to get into a Zen place. She got the small closed umbrella thing and pushed it up. Pushed it up very far. Then it opened and dug in and she pulled and it scraped and tore until out with some blood. CHRIST ON THE CROSS. I opened my eyes and saw HER smirking. What a bitch.

If only I could find a woman like that.

I limped out of there, hobbled to the car. I'd forgotten where I'd parked it. Found it. Got in and made it back to Edinburgh and waited. And the letter came. NHS envelope.

I went downstairs and the gay had a letter too. We got the chess set out...and the poppers.

He opened his letter first.

Dear Crispin Peploe,

We have read the first three chapters of your novel, Table Top Trouble, and would be pleased if you could forward the rest of the manuscript for our consideration.

Such luck.

'Nice one Cris. They'll publish that novel you know. Yes they fucking will.'

We both had a good blast on the poppers bottle, and I mixed wine with ale in a pint glass.

The Gay Downstairs   S A Tranter

I opened my letter.

Syphilis: negative
Gonorrhea: negative
Chlamydia: negative

The gay clapped his hands.

I downed the pint, chased him round the coffee table and squeezed his bum cheeks.

We were both in the clear.

For now.

Melissa Mann

Melissa is the head honcho of litzine Beat the Dust. An aptitude for words was apparent when in her first ever game of Scrabble she got 'turd' on a triple word score. Since then she has moved on to words in excess of four letters. For further details, the authorities have quite an interesting dossier on her or failing that visit www.melissamann.com.

Trick

Satan and the Bride of Dracula are standing in Terry's porch.
He is on tiptoes, looking at them through the spy-hole in his
front door. Terry is a small, middle-aged man with the
hunched shoulders of someone who has fallen short of himself on too many occasions. The girl he can see is about thirteen, ripe, in a long fitted satin-look dress. The little boy is
wearing a black suit and has two red papier mache horns
sprouting out of his ginger hair.

'Kids from the council estate,' he thinks. He rubs the five-
day old stubble on his wrecked face, reties his wife's dressing
gown then opens the door.

'Trick or treat!' shouts the girl, clinging onto the two-foot wig
towering above her head. It is shaped like a tiered wedding
cake, purple, glitter sparkling in the bright surprise of the
porch light. She nudges Satan, ''Rick treat,' he says, shyly,
waving hello with his fingernails. They look like puppies in a
dogs' home clustered round the cage door.

Terry clears his throat and hawks a mouthful of phlegm onto
the hall floor.

'Fuck... like I've really got time for this.'

Shaking his head, he plucks a can of lager from the dressing
gown pocket and takes a swig. He smirks and points at the
two kids with the index finger of his can hand.

'Fuck it, you know what, trick. Fucking trick. Gimme your
best shot, week I've had.'

The girl fiddles with the glass heart hanging between her new
breasts and puts an arm round her brother's shoulder. The
boy, wearing his sister's hand-me-down smile, looks up at
Terry, prodding his thin leg repeatedly with the fork-end of

the tail sewn onto the seat of his trousers.

'Go on then, trick. Do your worst, I deserve it,' says Terry, spilling lager down the trousers he's wearing under the gown.

'Shit, now look! Shit.' He swipes at his leg. 'So what's it to be then Satan and whoever the fuck you're meant to be... Mrs Satan? Ha!'

The boy pulls an egg out of his pocket and looks at his sister.

'A fucking egg. Is that it?' says Terry, bracing himself against the door frame. The boy looks down and starts to draw shapes in the dirt with his black slip-on gym shoe.

'That the best you can do, chuck a fucking egg at my door?'

The girl flinches as Terry reaches his hand towards her.

'See this, dug my own fucking grave with that this week.'

He holds it up to his face, looking at it from every angle.

'Wife left me on Monday cos she found out I went with a prostitute.'

He stares at the bitten fingernails, 'Didn't even know she was a pro so it shouldn't fucking count, should it?'

The Bride of Dracula has her arms folded now, head cocked on one side, one eyebrow trying to push up her wig.

'What? I swear to God I had no idea. I thought she was just a Strippergram. Well, Strippergran if I'm honest cos she was really fucking old...' Terry starts to laugh but it's a laugh that sounds like crying.

'They'd booked her for someone's leaving do an' we just got

chatting. S'how it always starts in't it. Then the chatting turned to looking. Next thing I'm fucking her in the Sales Director's office on that big fuck-off oak desk he's got.'

He reaches behind him still feeling the desk-top in his back.

'She's left me... fucking left me after eighteen years,' moans Terry, wiping his eyes with the dressing gown cord.

He swallows. Her going tastes like old lemons in his mouth. 'I'm sick of being a one-woman elastoplast, Tel,' that's what she said to me. What the fuck's that supposed to mean, for fucks sake?' He hangs his head and fumbles for the can of lager.

The girl takes the egg off her brother and looks at Terry, wedding cake wig listing dangerously to one side.

'I deserve a lot more than an egg down my front door, love.' He points at the boy's jacket pocket. 'You got a gun in there, son? A big fucker you could blow my head off with?'

Terry sees himself standing at the door of his bungalow in Wakefield, shouting at his own mouth. There is only one way back now but to Terry, it feels like the wrong direction.

'Well? You up for splattering my brains all over the porch, Satan or wha'? Go on, lad, do it for your Uncle Terry. Fucking trick and a half that'd be.'

The little boy's bottom lip is quivering. The tears in his eyes, threaten to curdle the white make-up smeared on his face. He reaches for his sister's gloved hand. The Bride of Dracula looks at Terry with hate's eyes then steps forward, smashing the egg as hard as she can into his crotch.

'That's for you and your free range dick, you prick,' she says, then sets off down the path, trailing Satan along behind her.

Ian Ayris

Ian is thirty nine years old and lives with his wife, Katie, and their three children, Mollie, Charlie and Summer, in Romford, Essex. A town where 'luxury' one bedroom apartments overlook boy-racer roundabouts and the streets are paved with chavs and dog shit. One day, Ian hopes to move.

Trains

She promised. Trish promised. She fuckin' promised. Get two single tickets. Aberdeen, she said. She reckoned we'd be in Jockland in three hours. No-one would find us there, she said.

Bloody trains. Fuck. Should've been here ten minutes ago. Kings Cross, fuckin' shithole this. All these faces. Blank. Looking up at this bloody board, waiting to be taken somewhere. Anywhere.

Me and Trish was teenage sweethearts, years ago now. Just kids really, seventeen, eighteen. It never worked out. Never does at that age. When things was really bad with Laura, I'd remember how Trish used to hold me, tell me she loved me. She was the first to do that, except me mum of course. When me and Trish split up, I met Laura, and well, that was that.

I bumped into Trish in the market a year or so ago. Her marriage was going nowhere, like mine. Had a bloke that hit her all the time. She said he weren't bad, just lost it every now and then. In my book, any bloke that hits a woman deserves a fuckin' good hiding. She begged me not to do anything, but I wanted to. I'd have torn his fuckin' heart out if she'd asked me.

Things with Laura was really shit at the time and I needed a friend. So did Trish. We sort of started seeing each other, on the sly, like. It was just mates first of all, you know, someone to talk to, catch up on old times. Cheered us both up, to be honest. One thing led to another and soon it was like the old days again. She made me feel so young. She made me feel like a man.

I'm sure Laura suspected something, she always did. The worse things got with her the more time I spent with Trish. Her bloke was pissed all the time, couldn't even be bothered to get off his arse to give her a clump any more. She'd had enough and so had I.

Telling Laura was easy. She knew it was coming. Had been for a long time. She weren't a bad old girl, not really. Nagged a bit, but then what woman don't? Ripped me to bits telling the kids. Lisa's little face, looking at me, smiling like she don't understand. Course she don't, she's only two, but I wanted to tell her anyway, do the right thing, you know. Sean was different. He's nearly seven. Cried his bloody eyes out, kept hitting me, little kid slaps, like a woman does. I put my arms round him and squeezed him tight, hugged him like I'd never see him again. Didn't want to let him go, not ever.

Trish weren't going to tell her bloke. Said she'd just pack a few things and go. She even bought the tickets. Told me she kept hers in a secret pocket in her purse, along with a photo of me. Then I gets this text from her this morning, says she can't do it. She can't leave him. I leave my fuckin' kids for her and she can't leave some fucker that beats the shit out of her. Fuckin' bitch. I gave up everything for her. Fuckin' everything.

Train's still not here.

Shit. Crowds moving, something's happening. Coppers. Bollocks. Loads of them. Probably went through her purse, found the ticket and the photo. Should've took my time, been more careful. Didn't think they'd get here this quick, though. Body must have still been warm when they found her.

<u>Darrell Irving</u>

Darrell has thus far completed one unpub-
lished novel 'On The March' - which has been
labelled 'Virgin Soldiers for the chemical genera-
tion' - from which this extract is taken.
Unfortunately he has recently been struck down
with the most unassailable type of writer's block
in existence. His name is James and he's one year
old now.

The Law Of The Jungle

Jimmy Reader was out of his box. He'd taken acid loads of times in the past but never three in one night, or was it four? The only thing he was certain of at that moment, was that he was off his face and his stomach was cramping up through laughing.

He'd met Bellsy and Don in town at four and as a special seventeenth birthday treat Bellsy had given him five acid tabs. The plan was to take two with them and keep the rest for next week, but that plan had been superceded in the time that it had taken them to drink their opening two pints and drop their first acid.

'Here Reader, drink that you lightweight.'

Reader took the pint from Don in an exchange which seemed to last for an age, but as he was always making out that Reader was a poor consumer of alcohol and drugs; he wasn't sure if it was the acid, or if Don was trying to take the piss.

'Don, what time's it like? I can't see me watch properly.'

'Fuck knows, but when Bellsy gets back from the bogs we'll go to Madisons. Wor Paul's on the door and he'll let you in, even though you look like a twelve year old puff.'

'Aye, you fucking wish huckle.'

Don was slow at the best of times but Reader's retort, disfigured further by the acid, simply reverberated around his head for a while, before dissolving and re-emerging as a signal from his brain to take another drink from his pint. As the lull in the conversation seemed to lengthen Reader again wasn't sure if Don was trying to trip him out. He'd done acid with these two a few times and knew from experience they could be hard work, so he was thankful when he spotted

Bellsy coming towards them, for bringing with him the opportunity to break the deafening silence.

'Here Don, here's the fucker now like. Look at his face; he looks like he's just had a blow-job in the bogs.'

'Well he was in there for a while and so was that big, fat bloke.'

Bellsy heard but ignored the insult as he put his arms around his two friends.

'Lads, let uncle Bells look after you. I've just swapped some bloke in the bogs five acid for two grammes of whiz.'

Reader didn't know what whiz was, but if Bellsy seemed happy with his deal then he knew that they'd be alright.

Since Reader had met him and Don through the Territorial Army he'd noticed that Bellsy was one of those people who normally came out of situations in a positive light. He was a shit soldier but he never seemed to suffer because of it, mind you in Reader eye's most of the blokes in there were shit soldiers.

Following this chemically induced train of thought he decided that it would be a good subject to broach with his friends.

'When you think about it the T.A.'s shit really.'

Bellsy looked at Don to try and figure out if the pair of them had set this up to try and trip him out, but Don's expression looked even more confused than usual. Confident that this wasn't some contrived sub-plot, intended to make him look silly, Bellsy carried on the conversation.

'Course it is but it's where we met up so it's not that bad is it? You don't get nights like this at the boys club.'

'Nah I don't mean like that, I mean with the standard of soldier in there. I'm only seventeen today and on our recruitment weekend I hammered everyone on the physical and mental stuff, grown men couldn't even do ten press-ups.'

Don's expression shifted from confused to defensive as he recalled having to stop after nine press-ups.

Reader continued, 'It makes me laugh when I hear all the politicians go on about how the British Army's the most professional in the world, well if the TA's anything to go by I'd hate to see the rest of the fuckers in action.'

Although he could feel and taste the acid strongly himself, Bellsy now realised that Reader was trying to enter into a serious discussion, on the merits of the British Army and their reserve counterparts.

'Reader man fuck off talking shite about the Army, people are only in it for the money.'

Reader knew he was tripping and he was sure that they would take the piss out of him but he didn't care, he wasn't joining up for the money, he was joining up to be the biggest, hardest, fastest, best soldier ever and he didn't care who knew it.

'I'm not, I'm going to be the best soldier there is. Fucking commando, para, S.A.S, I'm going to do the lot. Nothing's going to stop me.'

Bellsy knew that with Reader's current state of mind he could have a bit of fun with his young T.A. colleague, however he was also acutely aware that a young man as big and strong as Reader, coupled with large volumes of acid and drink, could lead to an extremely unpredictable and volatile situation. Bellsy considered Reader to be a good lad and he wasn't likely to kick off with a bit of banter, but after seeing the way that he had dealt with that lad in town last week, he had begun to afford him a lot more respect.

In those types of situation he would just leave the warring couple to it, but in this instance the girl wasn't fighting back, she was just being bullied. Bellsy had told Reader to ignore it, and thought that he had until the lad punched his girl-friend, then Reader was straight over and in a flash the lad was out cold. Bellsy couldn't help but think that maybe if Don had witnessed the event, then he wouldn't try and wind Reader up so much.

With this in mind he decided to pull the situation back around from the boring army talk.

'Well you can do that in a couple of months time when you join up with all the other Rambo's, but tonight we've got this whiz to get through.'

On that note Bellsy downed his almost full pint and the others followed suit, although Reader only had half a pint left, it seemed as though he was in a cartoon scene where he was drinking from a bucket with a never ending supply of liquid in it. It didn't help matters that it tasted bitter through the acid either and Reader couldn't help but notice Don's smug amusement at the fact he was last to drain his pint.

At the door to Madisons, Don's cousin Paul waved the three lads straight through. He was relieved that they'd turned up as early as seven o'clock with the state they were in and just hoped that they heeded his warning to sit out of the way in one of the alcoves while the place filled up.

Using his cousin's influence to get them into the club for free meant that Don was allowed to seize his chance to be momentarily elevated above Bellsy as the man about town. Ushering them to an alcove at the far side of the dark club, with a decent view of the dance-floor, Don took centre-stage.

'It's your round Reader.'

'Same again?'

'Aye for us, not sure if you'll want the same though.'

Reader could detect more of the same old repetitive Don banter about drinking prowess coming on, but he couldn't help himself biting.

'What you on about, I've drank more than you.'

'Aye liquid not beer.'

Reader didn't have a clue what Don was on about, even when they weren't on acid he made little sense and his jokes often led to embarrassing silences but then he noticed Bellsy starting to snigger and heard the alarm bells begin to sound.

'What you done like you cunts?'

Don almost couldn't answer through laughing, but he finally managed to spit his words out.

'That last pint we had in The Duke?'

As soon as Don mentioned that last pint, the memories of the sour, bitter taste flooded back into Readers mind and mouth, and it quickly dawned on him that someone had put something into his pint. He knew exactly what had been put in as well and he had to work hard to prevent himself from retching as he imagined the hot, yellow, liquid squirting into his drink as Don concealed it under the bar.

Reader kicked himself for leaving his pint with them, that was a mistake he wouldn't repeat, but now he needed to wrestle back some of the initiative or he'd be fucked for the rest of the night.

'Oh aye the Duke, it's shit in there like. My pint tasted like some fucker had pissed in it. You cunts.'

After what seemed to be about two hours worth of laughter, but was in reality only two chemically intensified minutes, Bellsy broke the tension.

'Happy birthday Reader, here have a dab of this whiz it's dead strong, you can feel it kicking-in through the acid.'

Aggrieved but hiding it well, Reader allowed his curiosity to become his main focus.

'Cheers Bellsy, don't take the piss but I've never taken whiz what does it do like?'

'Just like it says, it speeds everything up and as an added bonus it gives you the horn big style, even you and Don could score on the fucker.'

'Fuck off, even Don?'

Reader knew he'd replied with a lot of venom there and it was all directed towards Don. He'd done this enough times now to know that the score had to be evened up or face would be lost. Kicking off with mates wasn't an option and it wasn't his scene anyway, he had to be smarter than that. What he had to do was take all the abuse and wait patiently for Don to drop himself in the shit, and then when that happened, he had to be ready to pounce.

Once he got Don on the ropes he knew for a fact that Bellsy would quickly join in, simply because it would mean that he wouldn't be the prey himself. For Reader it was simple really, it was the law of the jungle, the survival of the fittest; all brought down to a new urban level, and he knew he was by far the fittest out of the three of them.

The taxi driver wasn't happy, he didn't like Gateshead at the best of times but he liked it even less when he had druggies in his cab.

'Here Bellsy, how many lasses are at this party like?'

'Fucking loads man Reader, don't worry.'

'It's me birthday man I've got to get a ride, especially with all this whiz in me.'

As the taxi pulled up Reader gave the driver ten pound in coins, the fare was only six but the driver had been okay with them especially as Don had tried to be cheeky when they first got in.

'Right then Bellsy, Don, that's two quid each for the taxi.'

Reader knew that they wouldn't contribute to the tip but he was feeling generous, and if he got a shag out of it then it was money well spent.

As Bellsy knocked on the door Reader couldn't help but notice that there wasn't any party atmosphere emitting from the house. The door opened to reveal two harsh, but attractive, looking women in their late teens to early twenties. Bellsy made the introductions.

'Lads this is Samantha and Donna. Ladies this is Don and this one's Reader, it's his birthday.'

'Is that the one with the muscles then Bellsy?'

Reader was happy to see that it was Donna, the better looking of the two, who had asked the question. He was pleased that Bellsy must have already mentioned him and his physique, although distracted for a moment through the acid; he surmised that only a queer fucker would go on about other lads like that.

Quickly snapping back to the present Reader addressed Donna's curiosity.

'Aye that's me, you can see them better with my clothes off like.'

'Oh is that right well I'll never know then will I?'

'I suppose you're right pet, it's my birthday not yours.'

Reader loved the banter and knew how to play girls like Donna. Although still young he'd had his fair share and his tactic was to humour them. Let them think that you're trying to court them and that you haven't really just turned up pissed, off your head and expecting a shag. In reality the truth was exactly that, but Reader knew that as long as neither of them acknowledged it then it was game on.

He wasn't being nasty to them, they knew and he knew that it wasn't going any further, and he would always be kind and friendly with girls he met, even in these sure-thing circumstances.

When Donna sat alongside him on the two-seat settee it confirmed to Reader that he was in pole position with her, and he was also joyous to see Bellsy getting straight into Samantha, leaving Don alone on the shitty dining chair. Don must have noticed Reader's triumphant leer as Donna sat next to him and after pondering for a while he spoke.

'Here Reader, I was keeping this for myself but you can have it, it's the last acid. You can have it for your birthday.'

In his mind Reader could still taste Don's piss from earlier and he'd done well to keep his temper all evening, ulterior motives raced through his head as he graciously accepted

46

Don's gift in front of Donna.

'Cheers Don, are you sure like?'

'Aye mate, help yourself.'

Don's plan was obvious to him; he could see that he wanted him to take the extra acid so that he'd be fucked leaving the way clear to sneak into Donna.

Reader had other ideas though.

'Cheers mate, but you don't mind if I share it with Donna do you?'

He drank in Don's look of defeat; his pathetic plan was now in pieces, he couldn't say no without offending Donna, who in turn gushed towards him.

'Oh thanks Reader, that's really nice of you.'

'Well you're a nice lass.'

'Shall we take it in my room then?'

'Oh right, that'll be great. I'll just get Don a can from the kitchen first so he's alright.'

Reader strolled through to the kitchen and he could feel the intensity of the hatred coming from Don; however he refused to reciprocate it and took the can of Fosters from the fridge and poured it into a glass for his friend. He wasn't interested in any petty conflicts, just happy in the knowledge that he was about to have a night of lust, heightened by the synthetic hallucinogenic of the acid.

'Here Don here's your drink, we're off to bed.'

As Don received the can he whispered in Reader's ear.

'You jammy cunt, she's meant to be well dirty.'

Within what seemed like minutes Don's last comment rico-cheted around his head as Donna ground her pubis into his mouth, only pausing her rocking motion to afford him a compliment.

'Reader, can I just say that I think you're really nice for shar-ing that acid with me and making sure that Don had a drink before we came to bed together and...ooh, yes that's it just keep doing that.'

As Donna climaxed she didn't notice Reader's muffled laugh as he thought of the long stream of piss, he'd squirted into Don's drink whilst in the kitchen.

Welcome to the jungle knobhead.

Craig Douglas

Craig has been writing sporadically since his youth. When he got sick of being a long haired student at Peterlee College he joined the Army and embarked on a ten year drinking spree. With his liver and kidneys just barely functioning he likes nothing more than going to Afghanistan and Iraq. When at home he assumes the role of husband and dartboard to a Russian.

<u>The Likely Lads</u>

'You couldn't fight your way out of a fucking paper bag!'
Jabba chanted then sat back in his seat grinning.

'Nah like. There were ten of them. Ahm tellin yer.' Seth
shouted back; bolting his skinny frame upright to defend
himself to the amusement of the group.

Jabba rode the wave of triumph. This fucker was biting like a
pitbull terrier 'Bollocks, I was there. A fuckin fourteen year
old.'

'Youse two are like fucking school kids - give it a rest man,' I
lightly rebuked the two of them, then focused on Seth, 'got a
light?'

'Ah divvent smoke.'

'Ah but if a bird asked yer for a light? What would you do
then, eh? You cannit strike up a conversation when yer
haven't got one can yer?'

'Nah. Ah divven't need a lighter. I can show any bird the light
at the end of the tunnel, when they get a piece of the python.'

Jabba couldn't resist the opportunity. 'That bird you went
with in the Navy Club said you had a party sausage and two
peas.'

'And which bird was that? Ah've shagged all the women that
work in there.'

'Fuckin' don't want to have.' Big George the Joiner hissed.
Heads turned and voices lowered.

'Apart from Sheila.' Seth quickly added. George nodded
across the room looking him square in the eye.

'So what chat up lines have you got then Seth? I'd like to learn some. You know, learn from the mentor.' Jabba changed the theme of the wind up due to the aggression he'd accidentally stirred up.

'Well. Ah divven't knah like.'

'Come on Seth' I urged. There was a rouse of encore from the rest of the bar as they all looked our way.

'Pet,' Seth began, looking at the faces around him, etched in concentration, 'do yer like chicken?' Their faces furrowed in confusion.

'Well suck me cock cos it's fowl'

*****

The afternoon sun drifted down behind the crest of the hill, silhouetting gravestones and projecting beams of yellow through the big window into the pool area wall.

'You know we've been talking all this time about these differ-ent things like it's fucking question time with all those nobs from London on it. How come you don't see any of those fuckers shopping up here in the local store?' Jabba asked.

Seth put his pint down and wiped his lips, 'It's the North-South divide. There's no jobs up here, Thatcher shut all the mines. It was difficult enough back then to get a job anyway never mind making it bloody worse.'

'So where's the line that says this is North and this is South?' I asked.

'That's something you have to find out yourself young Jedi. Go forth and explore.'

We looked up at the stranger who'd invaded our conversation. He wasn't steady on his feet, obviously been out all day.

'Youse cunts haven't seen the outside of this village have you?'

'I've been to Leeds.'

The old man laughed. He was skinny and his clothes were several sizes too big for him.

'You see lads. I'm a man of the world and can tell you there isn't a North-South divide. It's all up here,' he pointed a yellowing finger to his head. He seemed all fired up, full of passion - or maybe it was the ale.

'See for yourselves the next time you're down there.'

'Funny you should say that Grandad. Because we're off for the weekend on a caravan holiday down in East Sussex, that's in the South ain't it?'

The funny old man turned, finished off his drink at the bar and then left.

'What the fuck was that all about?' Jabba asked nobody in particular.

*****

We've been walking for about twenty minutes through this town and I've come to a conclusion.

What a fucking shithole.

Full of arrogant, self obsessed fuckers with more money than sense. Never heard of football. Only fucking croquet or carpet bowls. Only listen to Radio Four and drink red wine.

Sad bastards.

We're all about to head back to the caravan to get the fuck out of here when we see it. Like the blinding light of hope. A council estate. People actually do rent houses around here. Brilliant. That means a decent pub - likely to open all day. Sorted.

'This looks a bit better,' Seth goes indicating the raggy-arsed end of town.

They must've drafted in some right scruffy buggers here man. They must have pissed off the locals something chronic. If I were to get paid for collecting litter by the kilo I'd make a fuckin' bomb.'

'D'y'knah what they call window cleaners roond here?' Seth asks.

'No?' Me and Jabba say almost at the same time. Jinx.

'Fuckin' joiners man.'

'Aye alreet Seth. Cheers for that. You should be on the comedy hour y'doss twat.'

Seth claps his hands and rubs them. His eyes have that certain spark about them. I know this to be a sign for beer and that he's spotted the bar.

Jabba's seen it. He points a stubby, nicotine stained, penny dotted finger in the general direction of the pub. It stands alone. All the buildings around it have been demolished. The last stand. Ah can imagine the opening times on the sign.

'11 am - till - last man crawls out of our graffiti strewn, piss stained door'

'Howay then lads. What're we waitin' for?' Jabba yells, 'Set the fuckin' day away.'

He's off. It's the fastest I've seen the fat bastard shift since we got here yesterday. Set the day away alreet.

We're in for a sesh here mind. When Jabba sais that y'knah there's gonna be some serious drinking gonna happen. An' he can sup mind. We get closer to the pub and to our delight it's open. Fucking right an all. It's bastard half past twelve here. We'll' do some power drinking to catch up on lost time.

Things that make a pub.

1 A Decent Jukebox.

Mind 'ave seen many a dodgy jukebox. 'MC Dizaster and his rekking krew' - FUCK OFF.

Point to note. Always check the jukebox out before purchasing beverage in order to remove bad taste factor.

2. A Good Pool Table.

A pool table is always a good pool table when there's no fucker on it and there isn't a fucking queue of coins on it. End of.

3. Beverage.

Probably the most important factor a pub has. If the pub doesn't sell lager and has only Bitter, Real Ale (What the fuck's real Ale? Can yer get plastic ale?) and it's own local brand - GET THE FUCK OUT OF THERE!!

The bar is probably full of inbreeds donning Barbour Jackets, corduroys, expensive wellington boots, gun dogs, the odd stiff pheasant and a double barrelled shotgun.

These people are dangerous - they pay on average £3.50 for a pint.

4. Totty (or minge if you prefer).

This is an extra factor that will make your stay at the establishment that little bit more enjoyable - though I do stress this is not a necessary asset for a pub.

A nice wench behind the bar is alreet, but it doesn't matter what her coupon looks like. She could be fucking Pamela Anderson or Nora Batty - it doesna matter so long as she can pour a decent pint.

Watch our for young minge. They'll fucking bleed you dry and latch onto the next easy bastard once you're skint. Yer also get the ones that think they're something special. Ignore these stupid cows, they're just fools to themselves.

You'll also get some who'll flirt and once you start talking, you'll be thinking - fucking hell, I'm in here.

WRONG.

Her boyfriend happens to be the bouncer and he's happiest stotting your head off the four fucking walls. These tarts get off on violence - WATCH OUT.

So what was this place like?

Juke Box - Decent Tunes? Check.

Pool Table - only two on it. Check

Lager - Yes please. Check

The Barmaid however - WOULD NOT GET IT. No fucking

way. I just hope she can pour a decent fucking pint.

It's fucking dead mind with only me and the lads here.
Liven' the place up.

'Jabba, gis a quid will yer?'

I stick a couple of tunes on the juke box and walk over to the
Stegosaurus behind the bar.

'Pet. What time d'yer finish?'

'We're owpen aull day lav,' she whines, 'where yoo lot from
then eh? Scotland?'

Cheeky fucking hoor.

'WHERE?' Jabba shouts.

She notes the footy shirt and the look of shock on my face.

'So yoo guys are from Noocawstle.'

'Aye. Gods country.' I answer. She's getting too friendly for
my liking and I immediately change subject, 'can yer turn up
the volume? It's not like we're gonna disturb any of the
neighbours.' I say jokingly.

As she turns it up I decide to get another round in. I'm
halfway down me pint already.

Heading to the bog I see a condom machine near the urinals.
There's a notice which makes me laugh.

> If this machine is empty
> speak to the landlord.
> If this machine is full
> See the barmaid.

Nice touch but fuck off. She puts Quasimodo to shame in the ugly competition. Got a heed on it worse than the end of a witch doctor's stick.

Ah like this bar, it's a canny 'un. Ripped seats, fag butts on the floor, chewing gum to match. Graffiti on the tables, fucking brilliant. No bullshit with niceties. Tell 'em how it is an' pull nee punches. Belter.

'Killer. Fancy a game o' killer. Put a pund in. Eh?' I say to Seth 'n' Jabba.

'Aye alreet.......'

Halfway through the game about seven lads of varying sizes and ages walk in through the door. There's only one problem; they've got Southampton tops on.

'Oh when th' saints. Oh when th' saints go marchin' in I wanna be....'

Jabba gets all excited and broon aled up to fuck he jumps on the pool table and shouts 'Who's ARMY?'

I scream, 'TOON ARMY!!'

They're still singing. One of their mob is ordering the round. They're an organised bunch and they're taking it in good spirit.

Thank fuck.

'Fancy a game of Killer?' Jabba shouts across to them before they sit at the far end of the pub.

'How much is it mate?'

'A quid.'

'Olright then.'

'Just come back from a match then?'

'Yeh. We drew. Should have won.'

'Always the same case,' I say.

The young'un chirps up at this. He seems agitated and needs to get a word in.

'Facking cross bar. It hit the facking cross bar. Should've gone in.'

The kid must've been only seventeen. Young whippersnapper.

'Any other bars 'roond here? This is fucking boring.' Seth goes to one of them.

'It's pretty dead for a Saturday afternoon I know, but most of the regulars'll be coming back from the match to get drunk.'

Fuck.

He sees me glance at our footy tops. 'Y'should be alright. We only drew the game. Good bunch of lads.'

We all introduce each other and get on with the pool.

Half past two. Bags of time.

Set th' fucking day away.

Then I see them. Like a mass of zombies from a George Romero movie. Southampton supporters. About forty of them in line formation. Ready to attack the bar.

'Seth! Get th' round in. Pronto.' I shout at him with three fingers in the air. He understands. This signifies to get three drinks each as there is a rather large crowd approaching the pub. He's there in a second and getting served. He's also taking flak from an old goat in the corner. He must've disturbed his conversation with himself. The old fossil is pointing a bent finger at him. Seth's just saying, 'Aye, whatever mate. Aye...'

My shot next. He shoots. He fucking scores.

The footy crowd begin to assemble at the bar. One of them clocks the shirt and shouts, 'Facking Jordees...alright boyz?'

Jabba's chatting away to them while I'm checking the juke box out for decent tunes. England's Eyrie, The Beautiful Game....Stick that one on..

Something metallic catches my eye in the crowd and I see a wheelchair. It's covered in Southampton stickers and pictures of footy players. The driver of this automatic machine couldn't possibly hold a pint without spilling it. Whoever's designed this machine must have been a fucking genius. There's a place on the hand rest for a pint glass to be wedged in, this is not all either, there's also a long straw which goes into the blowkys pint. Fucking sorted. This lad's first priority. At least he's making the effort. He is as well, there's a pint of lager on his chair before anyone gets theirs.

Then I'm lining up to take my next shot.

Confidence.

You will go down my son. You will.

It rattles off the sides of the pocket and shoots out again. Eh!? But it doesn't stop there it goes on to tap off the yellow near the middle pocket and that one goes in.

'You spawny fackah.' Says this cockney 'saint' blowk.

I shrug my shoulders. 'I get more jam than Sainsburys after a few sherberts.' I say casually. YES. GOOOAAALLL.

At about four o'clock, my luck's ran out and I've ran out of lives. However Seth is up to his old tricks. There's only two left. Seth and Jambo (a saint) are the only two with a life left. One ball in play. Jambo is ready to take his shot. He wipes the sweat from his brow, composes himself. He's looking down the sight of his oak cue. Steadies his breathing. Just as he's about to strike.....

Jabba farts.

The entire bar reverberates with sound of his blaring arse and Jambo's only gone and slipped the cue off the white. Seth gives Jabba a wink of thanks before confidently knocking the last ball down.

'Get in yer bastard!'

There's a half pint glass full of pound coins and we split the cash three ways.

'Ahm paggered Seth,' I say to him.

'Y'not gonna flake out on us here are yer?' He gives Jabba a feigned concerned look. Jabba shakes his head in disappointment.

'Fuck off. I've never flaked.'

Seth goes to Jabba, 'I reckon he'll fall asleep by nine o'clock.'

'Nah. I don't think he'll go to sleep at all actually. I reckon he'll find it very hard to get to sleep,' Jabba says very confidently. What th' fuck does he know?

'Right lads we're off now to get some tea. No doubt we'll see you in here at eight then?' says one of the Southampton supporters to Seth.

Lethargy is starting to take precedence over my body and mind.

I'll just lie down here on the slashed rubber seats an' get me head down. A pint glass is shoved in front of my face. Literally in my face. Intended to rouse me to full alertness. Not so. I'm still fucked. Fucked... Bollocksed.... Can't be arsed.

Jabba's horrible slavering lips are next to my face. A shower of beer and cigarette breath.

'Get it down yer neck. Y'll feel a lot better.'

I take hold of the pint glass and....fuck it. I begin to pour the 'Fosters' down my throat. I'm looking at the glass, and it's empty.

I think Seth is saying something to Jabba, 'Awlreet noo. Just wait.'

I'm swimming and I'm not staying afloat. My eyelids close.

I FEEL FUCKING GREAT!

'I FEEL FUCKING BRILLIANT.' I shout jumping up in me seat, full pint glass in front of me.

Jabba gives me a wink of acknowledgement as I continue to rabbit on about something. I think I'm telling the both of them how much I love them as mates like and if they're in any kind of bother, I'd back them up pronto.

They're just grinning at me like Cheshire cats. Nodding with big cheesy grins. There is no cue for this, but they begin to howl with laughter.

When I see the small money bag with what looks like washing powder in it on the table I join them. Scheming bastards. They both knew I was beginning to flake. Good on them. These are MATES. Good lads.

***

'How many people can you fit into a pub? Is this an Anneka Rice's challenge or what?'

Seth's just come back from the bar which is currently four people deep.

What the fuck.

'Where's the rest of me pint?'

'It's on the fucking floor,' Seth replies in an irate manner. I'm on edge at his mood. He usually gets like this before he starts panelling some poor bugger.

He slams the three pints onto the table. Lager sloshing over the sides. He promptly turns and enters the fray. Jabba shrugs his shoulders. He knows exactly what's going to happen next. We hear a yelp, a scream. Then.

'Here, what are you doin' with my pint?' Sounds most definitely like a Southampton supporter. I can see it now. All his mates are going to back him up.

Jabba's going to join in.

I'm gonna have to.

We're going to get kicked into a hospitalised state.

Bollocks.

I can hear Seth's sarcastic, intimidating replies.

'As a member of Middlesbrough Football Club I'm confiscating it.' He promptly shouts back into the face of the owner whom we can't see through the drunken revelry.

Here he comes. Seth the Barbarian. No comebacks either. If it was me I'd have had the shit kicked out of me. He tops up all our pints to full ones.

'Fucking wuss.' Seth says as he takes a manly gulp.

Hello. Here's the Southampton supporters. There's a right crowd of them here.

'Are youse lot off to the Demi later?' The whippersnapper goes.

'Where? The Demi?'

'It's a nightclub. It's pretty good. Probably the cheapest beer and easiest women in town.'

'What about the minge state?' Goes Seth.

'Wall to wall.'

Me, Jabba and Seth give a cheer.

'When are youse lot plannin' t'gan down?'

'About half ten. They don't take anymore after eleven.'
I focus on the music from the band who've appeared now. It's alreet as well like. They may look like the residents of Broadmoor prison, but they can sing and then Jabba flinches, visibly fucking double takes.

'Aye up' he stands up and flicks his hair to one side.

'Jesus Christ.'

Seth's seen it and I'm looking at Jabba with a mixture of shock and disbelief.

'They call her Sasquatch. She'll eat yer for dinner and spit yer out.'

Sasquatch? It was a dancing, whirling, mushroom shaped woman. Rings on every finger, necklaces, bracelets, dangling earrings, the fucking lot. She'd have passed for a fucking Christmas tree. In one hand she had a drink. Something wi' coke in it and a smoking cigarette dangled from her bright red lips.

There was nee hanging aboot with that thing on the prowl for cock.

It's not long till we're on the streets. The Demi I've been told is down this street somewhere. Looks like fucking Beirut. I get the funny feeling that these Southampton supporters have lured us into a trap and are ready to shove us into an alleyway to stomp the shit out of us. I know I shouldn't think this, they've been excellent lads.

I start slashing down the street in mid stride. There's an art to this. Don't strain yourself and don't let the stream of piss slow down. You've got to get the right speed. Thus ensuring an enjoyable walk while pissing. We'd have piss trail competitions while on our way to the chinkies. It wasn't done in daylight. Fuck no. Get arrested by the filth if yer did that. Nah, this was about quarter to twelve, you'd see these trails of piss meander their way down the street.

Could dee with a chinkies mind. Fucking Hank Marvin.

'Where yer going mate? It's in here?' One of them says to me amid a chorus of laughs.

Jabba's zipping himself up and sweeping his greasy hair with the same hand. They were stood outside of what appeared to be a supermarket. Seth disappeared into a doorway. I hear it now, a dull throbbing beat from upstairs. We all herd about after paying a whole quid to get in. Welcome to the jungle. Here we go.

I'm no expert when it comes to discos, but I could safely justify wrapping a pool cue around every fucker in here.

'Full of fucking schoolies man.' Seth spat into my ear. Can't hear yerself think never mind talk.

'Look at the clip of this fucker.' He points to a young spunker making shapes on the floor, like he owns the place.

The saintsies had gone off to the other side of the crowd somewhere. Jabba's round with the drinks. Cheeky fucker's gone off somewhere. Ah'll have to watch that one - discipline's what's needed here.

Here we go. I am King of the Disco. It's all about attitude man. I think the billy's kicking in a second time round, must be doing fucking circuits of me bloodstream.

'BRING IT OAAN.'

I scream and begin to dance on the floor with two birds. One of them gives me a look and turns away from me.

Fucking lesbian.

I think the only way Jabba pulls is to get:

A. *The fattest pig in the club who can only be shagged from* *the rear*

or

B. *A semi-decent one, but who's completely rat arsed and would think he was a hunk.*

It looked like he'd opted for plan A. Good lad.

There's a couple of youths looking at us. Must be cos we're not from here - fucking inbred sheep shaggers. They're pointing at Seth who's busy firing some bullshit into a tasty bird up at the bar. She's sucking on a straw giving him the look she probably gives all the guys. 'Yeah whatever.'

I wonder what the doss Boro Mong is tonight? A McVities biscuit tester? An underwater wood welder?

I'm starting to get the butterflies in my stomach. I get them before any hassle. The local youth are fuelled up on alcohol and amphetamine and obviously angry at the 'Saintsies' draw today. It'll be our fault of course, because we're North of London.

I only notice now, because she's screaming obscenities at him. It couldn't be anything else from the look of her coupon. I'm not surprised. Seth the dirty bastard's doing his flies up. He must have pissed on the bar and on her.

The Youth Club probably see this as an excuse to kick off. There are about four of them. Chew 'em up and spit 'em out - nee problem. There are four of these fuckers, they look like clones, probably got the same father but different mothers.

'Jabba.' I scream above the din of the rave beat. He's busy tonguing this heffa's tonsils out. I've only just noticed - I thought it was the disco lights, but she's got green fucking hair. What is she? A fucking witch?

'Jabba.' The fat deaf fucker has finally heard me! He disengages from the elephant shaped thing. He spits out some chuddy (probably hers the dirty bitch) and says something. I think it's 'What the fuck?'

Ahm starting to get bad vibes here and I think we need to leave. I need to move.

I'm sticking to the floor. There's bits of chuddy and glass on the floor. I've just noticed this now. There's no way I'm falling over onto that. Jabba's here and he doesn't look happy.

'What?' He spits into my ear.

I point in the direction of the brawl. Seth's in trouble. The bird's proper shoeing him, heels and all - kid you not. She grabs his hair and tries to drag him. You've fucked up there Seth. One hundred percent. Just wait till I tell the lads about this back home.

Jabba to the rescue. He's picking Seth up while warding off the bird with one hand. The dirty bastard's groping her tits. I'd hate to think where those fingers have been. The elephant shaped witch is getting up from a chair. I think she's pulling up her knickers.

Silhouettes of manic ravers in awkward angles, like swastikas flickering on the floor. Frames are skipped, like those early silent movies. I need to move.

Events have gone up a gear. Jabba has one of the youths in a headlock. He's got this strange primordial look in his eyes. Go on son. He makes a run for the bar, using the kids head as a battering ram but loses his footing on a hypodermic needle and crashes into the floor like a downed rhinoceros.

This must be the cue, because the entire place has erupted

into a frenzy. There are things flying in the air. Must be bottles and glasses. The music has increased tempo and ferocity. The Prodigy are hurling out 'No Good' from door sized speakers. We can do this.

Maybe it's the billy, but I'm riding on the crest of something. Jabba's by my side. I remember playing the game Double Dragon when I was a kid at South Shields.

'Double Dragon.' I scream. Jabba's giving me a confused look.

What the...I've just had a glass hit me arm. Cheeky fuckers. Somebody hits me in the face and I'm wind-milling. There's fists, feet and fuck knows what else flying around us.

I'm hitting something and look down at it. It's Jabba.

He's seeing red and twats me one in the face. Fucker.

'Fucking get off Y'southern shite.'

I'm falling now. There's a void for a second then I'm bouncing down stairs. Shooting pains in my head, back and arms are making me howl.

Something heavy lands on my legs. 'Jesus.'

'He ain't going to help you son. Now get the fuck out. I knew you'd be trouble. Now fuck off up north where you belong you dirty northern monkey.'

It's the bouncer.

Jabba's puking, he's holding onto the fence of somebody unfortunate to live next door to this place. I think Seth's here as well, he's finishing off a bottle of Becks. I'm puzzled as to how the bottle survived, until I notice a solitary tab butt floating in it. He must have picked it up from the pavement. Dirty fucker.

'FAACK. Argh.' Seth's screaming and retching. He's hacking away at the cigarette to try and dislodge it from the back of his throat. I'm howling with laughter now.

It's then I remember what that old fart said to us in the Club last week.

'Well, did you find the North-South divide young Jedi?'

I ask the two of them. Seth's still hacking at the tab. Jabba's still retching, his face is the colour of beetroot. I sit down with my back to a fence, puke splashing behind me into the garden.

'It's all up there in your head.'

<u>Patrick Belshaw</u>

Although he has been published several times
Patrick still regards himself as a struggling writer.
His wife and most of his friends call him Pat,
which is defined in the dictionary as 'something
small, soft and smelly'

Are they trying to tell him something?

THE CROSSING

He was glad to get off the train. So many people. They couldn't all be making the crossing, surely? No, of course they couldn't. In fact, as he trudged out of the station towards the flower-bordered boulevard, the human stream had already begun to fan out, dispersing passengers in a dozen different directions. Silly man. There were a hundred and one other reasons for people to be out and about today. But it was easy to forget that - especially when your mind, your whole being, was focused on one thing, as his had been for weeks now. Ever since he had contacted the Agency to finalize the booking, he had been unable to think of anything else.

On the broad pavement of the boulevard leading to the port, he checked his watch and slowed down. He had plenty of time. Time to appreciate the Spring flowers, to smell the orange blossom, to enjoy the sun on his back and the gentle breeze on his face; time indeed, now that he was no longer being jostled, to relax his mind and his body, the way he had been instructed in the manual. He had always hated crowds: the noise, the press, the heat, the smell, the raw power and potential menace. It was a relief now to have a little space around him. Yet the crowds back there, on the train and in the station, had been a timely, if slightly uneasy, reminder that what he was doing was for the best. It hadn't been a simple decision. This was the land of his birth. He didn't want to leave. But one had to think of the future.

'Good afternoon, sir,' greeted the official behind the desk at Reception. He was a slightly-built, pasty-faced young man who looked as if he were in need of a break in the Sunshine Isles himself. 'Good journey?'

'Not really. Glad it's over. The trains were very crowded.'

'Always are, sir. Ever since petrol rationing. And road charges, of course. But at least it's safer crossing the street these days.' He paused, and for the first time he appeared to take note of his client. 'Anyway, you're here now. You came along Sunset Boulevard, I take it? Yes, most people do. It's the obvious route - and quite the best way, I always think, to complete this part of your journey. Fairly quiet this time of day, I assume?'

'Yes. Quite a relief. Those crowds made me realize suddenly how important...'

'... Of course, sir,' interrupted the official. 'I understand. You don't need to explain. Now, can I trouble you for your name and booking number, please.'

'Pendleton's my name. Christopher Pendleton. And my ...' he hesitated for a moment, before taking a piece of paper from his breast pocket and checking it, '... my number is VR389426. Sorry about that. I had hoped to memorize it, but they're such long numbers.'

'No problem, sir,' said the young man. 'I'd already got you on screen.' He spoke with the practised ease of someone who had followed the same routine, day in, day out, for longer than he cared to remember, 'and your mother's maiden name, sir? If you wouldn't mind? For security reasons, you understand?'

'Of course. Moffat - Moffat with a double 'f' and one 't'.'

'Thank you, sir, that's wonderful. Now...' he intoned, '... you left your main luggage at the station - yes? Good: don't worry, the Agency will take care of all that, and your hand luggage, sir? Packed by you, and you alone - yes? Excellent, sir. Can't be too careful, can we?' His smile seemed to writhe Heap-like across his face.

'Now, sir,' he continued, pecking at a pad with a long, bony finger, 'in a moment I will hand you over to Sharon who will escort you to the hospitality room in the First Class departure lounge. There you can help yourself to drinks and freshen up before being conducted to your berth.'

He hesitated slightly before proceeding. 'But first, on the subject of berths, may I enquire if you are still willing to share? If so, would you prefer to share with a male or a female?'

'Good Lord, I didn't realize I had a choice! Well, it might depend, of course ... but why not? Start of an adventure, and all that - so yes, let's take a chance. Bit of female company - not had much of that since...' He paused, his eyes becoming misty. 'Yes, might as well make the crossing as pleasurable as possible, eh? I say, this is quite a service.'

'Well, sir, we do try to please.' Had his lips moved towards a smile? Or was it another writhe? 'It has always been Agency policy,' he continued in a mechanical voice, 'to give special consideration to our VR-category passengers. As we see it sir your status deserves no less. So, a berth shared with a lady - yes?'

'Yes, I think so. Willing to take a chance, anyway.'

'Splendid, sir. You won't be disappointed, I can promise you. All Agency pairings are determined strictly scientifically, using the very latest sociometric and psychometric techniques. They come with a guarantee. In fourteen months, since we started handling retirement crossings, we have never had a single complaint.' He paused before proceeding with his well-rehearsed script. 'Well, I think that is all, sir. Except to say that I am glad to have played my humble part in processing your booking - and, of course, to wish you bon voyage on behalf of the Agency. The forecast, by the way, is for a very smooth crossing. So enjoy, sir. And perhaps you will now kindly follow Sharon.'

Sharon had short, blonde hair styled into a close-fitting helmet. She wore powder-blue trousers, with matching high-necked tunic, and white, soft-leather sneakers. Her oval face wore a fixed smile that looked as if it had been painted on with her make-up. Christopher tried to estimate her age, but gave up. She could have been anywhere between twenty-five and fifty-five: he really had no idea. Nor could he be certain, despite her name, that she was indeed a woman, for there were no curves to her slender form. There were no vocal clues to go on, either: she led the way in silence.

In the hospitality room, he poured himself a robust gin-and-tonic and took it with him into the shower. After drying, he helped himself to another drink of similar strength which he sipped as he dressed. This second shot made him feel warm and carefree, but it also made his head swim a little. If he had overdone it slightly - if he had poured the gin with a palsied hand, as his wife used to joke - well, so what...? He was, after all, about to embark on a momentous journey. What did it matter? What did anything matter? At his age, and at this time of his life, one took one's little pleasures at every opportunity.

The androgynous Sharon was waiting for him when he returned to the main body of the departure lounge. She led him towards a passenger conveyance that moved them silent-ly through a long, narrow passage-way whose oval walls were lined with fine-art prints. After two or three minutes, she sig-nalled him to step off the moving platform and to follow her along a short corridor. She stopped outside a white door where, with the touch of a finger, she activated a security pad. The door to his berth slowly opened inwards.

He turned to his escort, intending to thank her; but, totally fazed by her inscrutable silence, he found himself incapable of making a sound. It was unnerving: her body position, the angle of her head, the line of her smile - everything about her was just as it was when he first saw her. Nothing had changed. Except...? Yes ... as she was about to turn away, did he detect a slight hesitation? Almost as if she wanted to say something? He felt a sudden pang of compassion for her. Not much of a job, was it? Ferrying people you would never see again from one area of a terminus to another?

He produced a twenty-pound coin from his pocket and pressed the silver piece into her palm. With a slight inclination of her head, nothing more, she slipped the coin discreetly into the breast pocket of her tunic and departed.

Christopher's companion for the crossing was a woman named Hermione Darwin. They got on splendidly from the start; in their case, the Agency had got the matching process exactly right. Like himself, Hermione had opted for the voluntary package, as opposed to waiting, as most people did, for compulsory orders - so they had something in common from the start.

'Yes, I couldn't see the point of going on till I was forced out at seventy,' she said, in her down-to-earth fashion. 'I mean, don't get me wrong, I'm quite happy here - and I'm still sound of wind and limb, as you see - but a few more months are neither here nor there, are they? Might as well go early and qualify for the special concessions. Face up to it, old girl, I said. Country's too small: population's too big. Simple mathematics. Accept the inevitable. Jump before you're pushed'

'Yes, I had to give it a lot of thought,' said Christopher. 'It's a big step, after all. But my reasoning went roughly along the same lines. Anyway, decision's made now. So, what say we break into that champagne?'

Hermione was a heavy-featured woman, unfashionably dressed, with a large, intimidating frontage. Physically she was rather unappealing: not his type at all. But she had twinkling eyes, a keen intelligence and a fund of interesting stories. Born in Australia, she had come to England to do archaeology at Cambridge, and had then travelled the world on 'digs' - one of which, near Ephesus, had brought her brief fame on television. He remembered now: Digger Darwin, they used to call her. More recently, and with the same energy, she had taken up gardening, specializing in medicinal plants, including cannabis - which, she told him unashamedly, she had been taking with her food for years!

'Great for my arthritis - not to mention my dreams, and...' she twinkled, '... I happen to have brought some with me. Like to try a joint? Or would you rather have one of my little space cakes?' She giggled. 'I gave one to that creep on the desk, to have with his afternoon cuppa. So there might well be the odd mismatch this evening, I reckon. Serve the little bastard right.' She paused, seeing Christopher's face. 'Yeah, I know: not so funny for the couples concerned, maybe. But it'll make life interesting for 'em - and I'm all for that, eh?'

Christopher was about to respond when the door-bell rang. It was the waiter - all done up in bow-tie and tails: Hermione couldn't conceal her mirth - delivering the evening meal on a beautifully decked trolley, resplendent with covered silver salvers, silver candelabrum and a silver vase containing a single red rose, at the sight of which Hermione began to chuckle.

'Voila,' said the waiter, removing the lids with the flourish of a magician. 'As ordered, a 25:36:26 for madame, and a 25:58:26 for monsieur. Bon appetit.'

The fresh crab starter was delicious, they agreed; and they found it interesting that, as with the dessert, they had chosen the same dish. However, at times Hermione could hardly eat for laughing.

'A 25:36:26,' she kept repeating. 'I wish. At least, there was a time...'

Once the meal was over, she sat back and chuckled again. 'Can't get over it!' she said. 'The flunkey, the red rose, all that ceremonial crap - and for what: food by numbers, Chinese take-away style.'

'Yes, but the best take-away I've ever had,' said Christopher. 'I thought it was excellent.'

It was a different man who came to take away the trolley, but like his colleague he was impeccably dressed and professionally polite.

'I am delighted to hear that you enjoyed your meal,' he said, seemingly unaware of Hermione's lingering mirth. 'Now, please help yourselves to drinks from the cabinet. In five minutes time there will be a visual presentation on the big, white wall in your lounging area. I recommend it; it will tell you all you need to know about your destination. So, take to the recliners, lie back and enjoy.'

You're probably not aware of it - today's conditions in the Orchnae Channel are uncommonly calm - but the crossing is now under way. The captain reports from the bridge that the sun has just dropped down below the horizon, so be warned: it will turn a little chilly shortly. But do not worry: your berth is centrally heated, with the thermostat set to accord with outside temperatures. The heating will probably click on in the next few minutes. Please ring if you require further assistance. Otherwise, sit back, enjoy a drink, enjoy one another's company, enjoy the presentation; and if you happen to fall asleep - well, not to worry: we guarantee to wake you up in time to see the Retirement Isles come into view. Good night. If not before, I will see you on the other side.'

'Can't really fault them, can you?' said Christopher, after the door had closed silently behind the waiter. 'I know it's a bit over the top, some of it, but you have to hand it to them: it's all highly professional, if...'

'... if without soul, you mean?' said Hermione. 'All a load of
bollocks, if you ask me. Can't take it seriously myself.' She
smiled across at him. 'But at least the company's good.'

'Relieved to hear it, Digger Darwin,' he laughed. 'Now, what
say we have a double brandy - and maybe one of your space
cakes - and go through to watch the movie?'

'You're on,' laughed Hermione. 'You pour the brandies, I'll
get the cookies.'

The presentation, which began seconds after they took to
their recliners, was slickly produced.

'Welcome to Las Islas de la Jubilacion,' it began. 'The
Retirement Isles, as they are popularly called, are five jewels
set in the long, sparkling necklace of islands called on the
map, the Acherusian Archipelago, but more usually referred
to as Las Islas del Sol - The Sunshine Islands - because of
their tropical location. Formerly a Spanish possession, they
became part of the old British Empire towards the end of the
nineteenth century. Your accommodation - consisting, as
you see, of spacious bungalows built beneath swaying palms -
is located on the cool coastal fringes. It will be noted that
each bungalow is comfortably furnished, and fully-equipped
to the highest modern standards, and - how about this, folks!
- each unit of four shares this attractive leisure pool.

All provisions are brought to your door in these quaint elec-
tric floats - so no noise, no smell! - and full medical care is
available 24/7. You need never leave the complex - your
home, indeed - unless you wish to; but if you want to be
adventurous, the islands offer a varied topography and plenty
of places of interest. So, you lucky people, imagine yourselves there already - reclining by the pool or on the beach, a
sun-downer in your hand, a gentle breeze on your cheek, listening to the sound of the sea breaking gently on the shore,
with not a care in the world...'

At this point Christopher turned to Hermione, fully expecting to receive an explosive retort along the lines of what bland, promotional pap to be feeding intelligent people who still had enough teeth to chew on more demanding fare, but she was fast asleep.

'Night, Digger,' he whispered. 'Sweet cannabis dreams!'

He settled back in his recliner and returned his eyes to the screen, in time to see yet another strand of silver sand lapped by a pacific, gently susurrating sea. The sea's peaceful sibilance was all around him now. It seemed to come through the very walls themselves, reminding him oddly of the gasfire he and Liz used to have in the early days of their marriage.

'Ah, well, Hermione,' he said quietly, closing his eyes. 'You're right. Time to give way to sleep. See you in the morning, old girl. See you on the other side.'

Fiona Glass

Fiona lives in Birmingham with one husband, several cats and far too many spiders, in a
pointy Victorian house which fuels her love of
ghost stories. She writes darkly humorous fiction,
and often puts the people she meets in everyday
life into her stories. You have been warned. You
can find her website, with details of the work she's
had published, at www.fiona-glass.com.

Rock and a Hard Place

It's all old Hinchcliffe's fault that Jed Lemmon turned gay.
There I was lounging in bed one Sunday afternoon, hand
resting on some blonde babe's left boob, when there was pan-
demonium downstairs and before I knew it he was banging
on the bedroom door. That kind of pissed me off. I mean, I
know he's my manager and I gave him the key myself, but us
rock stars deserve some privacy - even washed-up old scrotes
like me.

I patted Suzie on the rump and sent her home, then scraped
my jeans off the bedroom floor and dragged them on. A quick
swig from the flask I'd hidden by the bed and I was more-or-
less ready to face the old man.

'Wotcha Jed,' he said, grinning from ear to ear and jabbing
me in the chest. 'How's things with you?'

'Oh fine, just fine,' I mumbled, trying not to watch as Suzie's
Jeep sped off bad-temperedly down the drive. 'What can I do
for you, Mr H?'

It was the usual - of course it was. He dropped the bonhomie,
even as he dropped his rump into an over-padded chair.

'Business as well as pleasure, Jed. Records, to be precise.
We're not selling enough. Sales are down for the seventh
month in a row - nobody's buying your stuff.'

I took my time lighting a cigarette. 'I'm sorry, Mr H. I've
done everything you said. I can't think of anything else.'

Well, why the hell should I? It's why I pay him a bloody great
wad of my earnings every month.

'I know - and I'm proud of you. But don't worry, I've had a
brainwave.'

My heart sank. Great bloke, old Hinchcliffe, and I couldn't have got where I am without his help. But his brainwaves are notorious. We'd already had the Jed novelty hats and the posters given away with Choco-flakes, and as for Jed Lemmon dressing up as an orange to advertise yoghurt - I'd had nightmares for months.

His jaw developed a horizontal crack that might have been a smile. 'It's simple. We tell the world you're gay.'

I inhaled the cigarette. 'You what?'

'It's fashionable these days - there's a lot of potential in the pink pound, and the girlies love it too.'

Try as I might I couldn't work that one out. Still, I'm an easy-going sort, I'll agree to almost anything to keep the peace. 'Well, if you say so. What d'you want me to do?'

'Stay put,' he said, waving an airy hand. 'There's someone I want you to meet.' He heaved himself off the chair and waddled out, and when he came back he had someone in tow. 'Jed, meet Simon.'

'Hi Simon,' I said without looking up. Then I did, and forgot to close my mouth. That was Simon? He was.... remembering, I clambered to my feet and stuck out a hand.

'Pleased to meet you.'

'Hello, Jed,' he said, and even his voice was... and his eyes were feasting on me. I didn't know where to look.

'Fancy a beer?' It gave me an excuse to get one too.

'Love one. Thanks.' He took the bottle and made sweet love to the neck with his mouth.

After long moments I tore my eyes away. 'So how's he going to help us, Mr H?'

'That's easy son. He's going to be your boyfriend.'

I choked again, on the beer this time. 'Oh yeah?' I croaked. 'And what does Simon think about that?'

'I don't mind,' said Simon, with a smile that - almost - made everything all right.

Soon after that Hinchcliffe left us alone, with a remarkable show of tact. The next few minutes were hell on earth - I don't remember being as embarrassed as that even when I was in my teens. Possibly because I was too busy fighting off the groupies and planning my next world tour.

In the end we got ourselves past the 'How are you? I'm fine, how are you?' routine, and I sat us down with another beer and took the plunge.

'So how do we play this, then?'

'If this is a publicity stunt then presumably we need some publicity.... If you're up for it, that is.'

I fiddled with the bottle cap. 'Ah, well, you see that's the problem right there.'

'Oh? Okay, if you don't want me we can always find someone else.'

Talk about getting the wrong end of the stick. Just how did I go about explaining that all I wanted was to drag him to the floor and shag him into the middle of next month? I could have come right out and said it, I suppose, but there are two things wrong with that. One, I've protected my image pretty damn carefully all these years and he might run straight to the nearest Sun reporter the minute I spilled the beans. And two, I wasn't sure he liked men. Hinchcliffe could have picked a straight guy on purpose, knowing it was all a hoax. What a bloody mess. In the end I muttered, 'I suppose we could start at the clubs. Know any good ones?' which at least gave nothing away.

He paused long enough to make me think he was having second thoughts. Then, 'Yeah, Pink Peach is supposed to be all right.'

'Sounds good. Friday okay?'

'I'll pick you up at ten.'

And getting myself a boyfriend was as easy as that.

* * *

Friday duly arrived, and with it Simon, driving a scarlet Porsche with a number plate that read S-1-MON.

'Like the car,' I said, more to break the ice than because it was true.

He held open my door for me and pulled a face. 'My, er, ex bought it for me. I'm not into all this personalised crap but I can't afford to replace it. Besides, it goes like a dream.'

He proceeded to demonstrate, at speed and with a howl of exhaust that would have woken Sleeping Beauty herself. There went the neighbourhood, I thought as I hung on. Not that I like Solihull, never have - it's too posh by half. The residents manicure their drives and shampoo and set their lawns, and look down their noses at me. Perhaps it was time to move on. I've always fancied a nice little terrace myself, but Hinchcliffe won't hear of it. 'Got to act the part,' is his favourite motto right now.

Broad Street, as ever, was awash with kids - I swear they get younger every week. The good thing was they were too young to recognise me; I may only be forty five, but to teenagers these days that's as old as woad. The bad thing was they didn't recognise me. Well, there's not much point doing a publicity stunt if no-one knows who you are.

Pink Peach was stuck away down a back alley and had a giant peach above the door. The stuff of nightmares, poised to fall and roll off down the street, crushing unfortunate teenyboppers in its path. Except they're not called that now, are they? Inside it was much like any other club except that the girls were boys. Music thumping, too much neon and the lights down low so the stains don't show. The music was mostly eighties classics (which is a contradiction in itself) and I winced as Simon led me in just as Tainted Love blared out.

'That's so stereotyped it's untrue,' I muttered, kicking a handy bar stool into place and parking my behind.

'What's up with you?' yelled Simon, handing over a beer.

I couldn't be bothered explaining, and anyway the music was far too loud. I shook my head, knocked back the amber nectar, and prepared to be entertained.

Except it wasn't very entertaining, really. Guys danced with other guys, or lined the walls for a snog, but it was all a bit 'been there, done that', if you know what I mean. I'd expected more from my first visit to a gay club, and began to wish for an alien invasion, or a joint, to liven things up.

Eventually the beer reached the parts that all beers reach, and I headed for the loo. After tacking across the dance floor I thrust open the door to the gents - and came face to face with myself. Well, that's okay, I've seen mirrors before, except this reflection wasn't doing the same things as me. It was smoking, for a start, where I'd left my fag in the ash tray on the bar. And I'd never owned a shirt in that bilious shade of green.

The reflection grinned, showing a gold tooth I didn't know I had, and spoke without my lips having moved. 'You're good. Which number are you?'

I grinned weakly and made a bolt for the nearest cubicle, and it was quite some time before I ventured back out. Well, you hear some bad things about doppel-gängers, and I didn't want to put it to the test. But the instant I emerged from the gents it happened again. This time my double was taller and wearing a yellow top so tight it highlighted every rib. Worse still, he had his arm slung round yet another clone. Everywhere I looked there were copies of me and it was starting to mess with my head. I staggered back to the bar on weakening knees, fortified myself with another swig of beer and hissed in Simon's ear.

'Let's go somewhere else. This place is seriously weird.'

He looked at me as though I'd sprouted two more heads, but all he said was, 'How d'you mean?'

'I mean I keep seeing myself. It's not a pretty sight. I think I'm cracking up.'

'Oh, that.' He grinned and waved a cocktail umbrella towards a poster on the wall. 'You mean the contest. I thought it would be a laugh.'

I squinted at the sign; I should wear specs really but don't like the line across the top of my nose. Finally the Red Sea of bodies parted long enough to give me a clearer view.

TONIGHT - ONE NIGHT ONLY
GREAT PRIZES!!
JED LEMMON LOOKALIKE CONTEST
BRING A FRIEND

And beneath all that there was an oldish photo of me, from the days before the crow's feet started to grow legs. I stared at myself for a while, until light dawned at somewhat less than the speed of sound.

'You're kidding. When did I get popular enough for a looka-like contest?'

'You're the one that's kidding, right? Jed, you're a gay icon - have been for years. Don't tell me you didn't know.'

'But I'm not....' I gave up. Pretending to be gay was bad enough. Pretending to be a straight guy pretending to be gay was hurting my head so much my hair was falling out. Even more than usual, that is - at this rate I'd be bald by two am. The music had been a little quieter but now Frankie's 'Relax' was belting out and there was no way I could make myself heard. 'Come outside,' I mouthed, and tugged Simon off his stool.

Outside a huddle of smokers perched on the steps, puffing blue fumes into the sky. I joined them and lit up, taking the smoke down deep into my lungs and savouring the hit. It was starting to spit with rain, but after the heat and crush indoors the air was blessedly cool and it felt good to be alive. Until I saw Simon's face.

'If you're upset we can go somewhere else,' he said, squinting at me unhappily through the smoke. 'I just thought it would be good, because if you have second thoughts about this gay thing you can always say it wasn't you.'

I waved the cigarette. 'Don't worry, I just wanted a fag. And anyway, it's like being pushed over the Niagara Falls in a bar-rel in there. My hearing's crap at the best of times. Comes of sharing a stage with all those speakers for so many years.'

'Of course.' His face cleared. 'So, are you in the contest?'

'Why not? Should shut old Hinchcliffe up at any rate.' As Simon said it would be a laugh - and what could possibly go wrong?

I found that out at midnight, when they lined all the competitors up along the bar and proceeded to hold a vote. I'd watched the same sort of thing on Pop Idol from time to time but never realised before how difficult it was. You'd think getting up on stage in front of a stomping, yelling crowd was bad enough but this was much, much worse - after fifteen minutes of waiting I felt like I'd been peeled.

The other contestants all had party tricks - some played long solos on air guitar, some mimed pretending to sing. When my number was called I went absolutely blank. I shuffled two steps forward, nodded a couple of times, and shuffled back again, hitting my elbow on the bar. By the time I'd finished swearing and seeing stars, the compere had moved on, and I'd had no time to count the show of hands. 'How did I do?' I yelled to Simon, who was in the front row, but he only shrugged and grinned.

He grinned even more when the results were announced because we found that I'd come third. In a lookalike contest of myself. To make matters worse, the winner was the bloke in the terrible green shirt.

'It's all right for you,' I said sourly, watching as he creased at the waist. 'You haven't got to live that one down.'

'Don't worry, nobody will ever know except me and you.'

'That's what I'm afraid of - you'll hold it over me for years. If you ever breathe a word of this, to Hinchcliffe or anyone else, I'll tell the world you chose that car and the number-plate yourself.'

That sobered him for about twelve seconds, then he started

again. This time he was howling and I wondered when I'd missed the joke.

'What?'

'It's nothing.'

'It must be something or you wouldn't be wetting yourself.'

'No, really, it's best you don't know.'

I took him outside again at that, torn between wanting to kiss him and smack that annoying grin off his face. The threats didn't seem to be working so I changed tack. Grabbing handfuls of his shirt I pushed him against the nearest wall and shoved my tongue down his throat. He clearly wasn't expecting the all-out attack, but the protesting squawks soon faded and the struggles died away. When we came up for air he was smiling again, but in a very different way. That'd teach him, I thought with a touch of pride, but the fall that followed was long and very hard.

'I probably shouldn't tell you,' he said. 'But the reason I was laughing? It was you talking about telling Hinchcliffe. Jed, he already knows.'

I don't know if it's all the weed I've done but my brain is always a minute behind everyone else. I hadn't a clue what he was on about, and said as much.

'He set the whole thing up. Who d'you think organised this contest for tonight?'

Why do these things always happen when I'm smoking a cigarette? I'd just lit up again and this time my tonsils caught fire. By the time I'd put out the flames and finished coughing up smoke it was all I could do to wheeze, 'No shit?' And then, as light began to dawn, 'Are you saying he knows I'm gay?'

'Yup. Has done for months, if not years. He's a good bloke, Jed, and he loves you like a son. Well, perhaps more like a younger brother given your relative ages, but you know what I mean. He talks a lot about promotion and sales, but all he really wants is for you to be happy.'

I thought about the orange. 'He's got a funny way of showing it, then. And anyway, how come my manager knows so much about the gay scene?'

I thought I was going to have to kiss him again, but in the end he replied. 'Ah. I was hoping you wouldn't ask me that. Michael - Mr Hinchcliffe - he's my ex.'

'Hinchcliffe bought you that car? Jesus, my sales must be better than I thought. I can stop all this gay nonsense now and go back to being myself.'

Was that a pout underneath his hair? 'I'm rather hoping you won't.'

It was way too soon for that sort of commitment, and anyway I'd just had the night from hell. 'Get me home before I conk out,' I said. 'I've had about as much as I can take.'

It was hardly a declaration of undying love, but he seemed pleased enough, and smiled as I took his hand. But when we got back to where we'd parked the car he broke the contact and strode ahead.

'Hey, hang on. It should have been right here.... Some bugger's nicked the car!'

<u>Martin Reed</u>

Martin's work can be found in obscure places, online and off. You just need to know where to look. But that's the problem with obscure places, isn't it? Right now he's thinking sod it to obscurity. This is the year to sell out and write about boy wizards and spunky thirty-something heroines with diaries that make millions. Or not. Sod it. Martin blogs at worded.co.uk.

Sheena up a mountain wearing flip-flops

Don't laugh like. Me and Sheens camping in Snowdonia. Doing the big friggin outdoors thing. Me and Sheens in a field in the piss friggin rain.

Friggin 'ay.

I mean why on earth are we doing this? With all that shite blowing up the other night we just can't wait to get away. The tent's coming down after I've polished off this tinnie and then we're out of here on the twelve fourteen. At my age you'd think I'd be too old to get homesick, but I welled up last night when I thought of the flat. I'm even missing ruddy Liverpool. In a way.

Not as much as we're missing our Danny mind. Sheens has spent most of the trip pining for the little man. He's all right but it's what parents do isn't it. You worry for him when you aren't with him, even though you know Lydia Worsley's looking out for him and she'd never let anything happen.

I wonder what a one year old would make of this. The whole friggin adventure of tents and rain and mountains. He'll be off for his nap about now, just starting to fight it, shaking his head. No way, I'm not tired like. Little bugger.

Of course it's just as well our Danny isn't here. Crazy women shining torches in your tent at three in the morning doesn't exactly make for a good night's sleep.

***

It's coming up on half past ten. Always a bad time for Sheens. Just one of those things. She goes into herself around this time, then slowly comes back up in time for lunch. I know there's nothing I can do. She just has to ride it like. But I unzip the tent enough to squeeze my head in. She's curled up on the floor in her sleeping bag, clothes piled thick on top.

'You all right, love?'

I know she isn't. She curls herself tighter.

'You cold, love? I know how you're feeling like. My bollocks are like ice cubes.'

I'm about to leave her but I think I know what she's thinking. 'Listen, Lydia Worsley won't let anything happen to him. He's all right, our little man.'

She uncurls her head for a moment and whispers something. I can't quite hear but I think she says that Lydia Worsley doesn't always know best. There's no answer to that, so I just say, 'Keep warm, love, I'm out the front having a fag and a tinnie if you need me.'

I zip her back in, safe. There.

***

It was a different picture this time yesterday morning. A bit weird like. My head was dead heavy when I woke, what with psycho woman in the night and a tin too many the day before. It took me a while to realise Sheens wasn't there and when I did I almost panicked enough to sit up. Then I heard her singing outside. Singing like. Perfect Day. I mean where the frig did that come from?

'You all right, love?' I called and she like yelped, ripping open the zip and she came diving in, still in her jammies, landing on top of me soaked through with rain, giggling.

'We're going up a mountain,' she laughed.

'The frig we are. It's pissing down.'

'Look,' she said, poking her finger into the ceiling of the tent so it squashed against the top layer. Rain from outside trickled down her hand onto her arm, pooling at the elbow before dripping onto my sleeping bag. There were wet patches all over her side of the tent. I think she'd been doing this all night.

She said she wanted to do the big mountain because it was something she'd never done before, and she might never have another chance or get hit by a meteorite, and besides there's a café on the top where we can get a cup of tea and a sarnie.

I told her she was mad as frig but she could have her mountain. So off we went.

***

On the bus on the way up to Snowdon she was like a schoolgirl. In the two years I'd known her I'd never seen her like that. She so often seemed distant, especially since Danny was born, making me feel like I'd fallen for someone through frosted glass. But yesterday morning there was something in her that seemed like she'd turned a corner. Something girlish like. Something fun. I watched her as she stared wide eyed out the window.

'Just look at that sky,' she said, 'it's swallowing mountains whole.'

She told me when we first met that she was complicated. She told me there were things about her I didn't want to know, that I couldn't ever know and when she said it like that of course I didn't want to. I never understood until everything came out the day Danny was born, the day we met Lydia Worsely.

Things have a habit of coming out. Like they did at the hospital. Like they did here the other night.

***

We'd been getting back to the site after lunch and seen this middle aged couple setting up their tent next to ours. I said hello to them and the bloke nodded but his missus didn't say nothing. She just went all nervous like and disappeared to the toilet block.

'Your missus a bit shy like?' I asked. But the bloke just shrugged.

We didn't see them again all day, then in the night just as I was managing to get some sleep at last I was woken by shouting and an angry unzipping next door.

There were voices coming closer, his and hers, babbling.

'What are you playing at?' came his voice. The bloke from next door.

'It's her, I know it is,' came hers.

'It's the middle of the night.'

'Let go of me.'

'It's the middle of the night, please.'

'It was her, in the flat opposite Rita's, don't you know what she did to them?'

All the while quick jerks of torchlight played on our tent walls, steadily getting brighter.

Another angry zip. Ours this time. Someone's eyes shining in for a moment before I was blinded by the torch, shining first at me then Sheens, still asleep.

'It's her,' screamed the woman, it's her, 'look, let go of me. That bloody monster.'

I was so dumbfounded I couldn't say or do anything. I hadn't a clue whether it was real or a bad dream, which is probably just as well because my usual plan is to slap first and think later.

As Sheens stirred I could hear other voices outside. The camp site was waking and the woman must have realised because she moved away from our tent, screaming the worst things, all the terrible horrible things I had never wanted to know, all the things they'd said about Sheens back then, all those friggin awful truths. I didn't dare go outside.

I looked at Sheens, lying there. She was taking it all in like. What a thing to wake to. She closed her eyes and rolled over, the accusing voices still rattling through the rain. How could she ever hope to sleep with that going on? Although maybe it was no different to always, except the accusing voices usually come from inside.

***

On the mountain, it didn't occur to us until we'd been walking an hour that perhaps we hadn't come best prepared. Sheens just laughed as she said she should've brought her trainers. I pointed out that I was friggin soaked; that I was getting wetter and colder. She told me to stop whining and the only reason I did was because it was just beautiful seeing her like this. We'd passed half past ten a while back and she hadn't done her usual.

I told a sheep staring out from behind a rock, I've never known her so happy.

The sheep carried on staring.

Mind you, it wasn't just the sheep staring at us. In spite of the crappy weather there were still plenty of others heading up, overtaking us with their backpacks and woolly socks. They nodded as they passed each other, saying its a bit of a rough day for it, all knowingly like. Then they'd spot us stumbling along and you could see them tutting, not so we could hear, but enough so we knew they were doing it.

'That pisses me off.'

'Just ignore them,'she said, 'they don't matter.'

She walked on and when I looked round again we had the mountain to ourselves.

You'd think we'd have got used to being judged after everything that's happened, but it still riles me.

***

The first time I met Lydia Worsley was at the hospital, six hours after our Danny was born. She spoke gently, quiet like. I could hardly hear over the din of the ward so she had to say it twice. She said, 'in a few minutes you probably won't trust me, but you need to know I'd like to help you.'

***

I stood at the edge of a drop which fell away into mist and nothingness.

'Tell your mam I saved your life, 'Sheens laughed grabbing my arm, pretending to push me over. Then she pretended a bit more roughly and grinned, 'tell your dad I didn't.'

She ran off up the slope shouting something about the first

one to the top, her words drowned by the wind and a fighter jet screeching overhead.

***

When Lydia Worsely arrived on the ward I think Sheens had seen her coming and knew right away what she was. She started to shuffle herself off the bed towards our Danny, asleep in his cot, then stopped suddenly, holding her stitches. She wasn't ready to move that quick.

Clueless me though, I just said, 'Hello, how's it?'

What else could I say? I couldn't work her out. I just thought she was one of those hospital visitors who trundle round the suicide attempts trying to perk them up.

***

It was half past ten in the morning when Lydia Worsley took our Danny away, and she didn't look back. I couldn't even see his face to wave to him. I stood at the foot of the bed, watching our little blanket bundle glide out of the ward, aware of a quiet sobbing behind me which I couldn't bear to face. I could only look at the door as it shut, hiding our Danny from view.

***

The mountain was all closed when we got to the top and Sheens went off on one. The good time was officially over. There was no café, just fog, wind, rain and a building site. A laminated sign strapped to a six foot fence said the old café had been trashed and the new one wouldn't be open till next year.

'Fuck.' Sheens rattled the fence, then kicked it.

'Hold on, love. Don't spoil it now. There might be something else.'

'What? You think they'd shove two fucking cafés up here?'

'I don't know like. I thought there might be a little gift shop or something. You know. Postcards.'

'Fuck off,' she muttered marching back into the wind. I nearly had to jog to keep up with her.

'Come on love,' I called after her. She was climbing again but up steps this time, to the real summit and when I caught up with her she was grasping a round waist high stone plinth, as though the wind would have taken her if she hadn't clung on with everything she had.

***

When Lydia Worsely told me everything I couldn't believe a word. I needed to hear it from Sheens.

'What did you do to them, your other kids? Why did they take them? What Lydia Worsely told me, Sheens, is it true?'

It's a year later now and she's still figuring out how to answer me, which suits me in an odd sort of way. Until she tells me herself it's just other people's words and I can half convince myself they might not be true.

She's shown me photos like. Of a happy family. The kids. Christmas trees. Her ex. All the things I know we'll never see with Danny. But when I asked her why she never mentioned it before, she just said she needed someone who didn't know.

We stood shivering at the top for ages. Just staring out into the freezing friggin fog, wind blowing right through us, right into our bones. Completely friggin relentless. But it was where we belonged for that moment, Sheens gazing out into the nothing, and me not sure whether to comfort her or back off, not sure if the trickle on her cheek was a tear or just rain. But there she was, the daft friggin bitch, on top of ruddy Snowdon wearing a t-shirt, shorts, a Woolies kag and a pair of pink flip-flops. The state of us.

I wanted to say something but before I could she turned to me, and I saw they were tears, and she just said, 'Why did they do it again? Why didn't you make a fucking difference? Why weren't you fucking enough?'

***

When Lydia Worsely spoke to me nine months ago she said I had a chance to make things different. We'd been meeting Danny a couple of times a week at a drop-in centre and apparently they'd been watching me.

'You need to know that it isn't you we're worried about.'

This was Lydia Worsely all over: everything she said you needed to know. She said I could change things for Danny, if only I wasn't with Sheens.

I asked, 'How would you know I could change things?'

I can't remember how she answered.

***

So right then. We're all packed and the bus heads off in ten minutes.

I don't think we'll be doing this again, so with the tent in its bag I look around for a hedge to dump it. It was only seven ninety-nine from Argos, cheaper than the pitch so, you know, no harm done. But then I see this kid, must be about eight or nine, standing by his tent a few down from where we are, staring at us. His mam and dad will have warned him to steer clear of the child molesters in the tent at the end, and he most likely wants to see how many friggin dead babies we've got in our bags.

You can't blame the kid but it's that being judged thing again isn't it. The thing that no matter how hard I try I can't quite get my head around. And you know what, it friggin fucks me off. So I grab the tent and walk at him, across the yellowed grass where mad bitch had been, on past the others, staring the lad out as I go. Then just as he looks like he'll bolt I slow down and lob the tent at him. It lands at his feet with a wet thud.

'Pressie for you, son. Get a girlfriend and take her away for a few days. It's a laugh.'

I turn back and make for Sheens waiting by the bags. She struggles with a smile for a moment but it's a bit too early, so it fades.

***

On the way down the mountain yesterday there was a moment when the cloud around us thinned and we could see for miles. We watched while it lasted. Just for a minute.

Dorothy Crossan

Dorothy is interested in consequences and what happens when people ignore them but when a deadline looms she will write about anything that is not nailed down. She dabbles in poetry but in consideration of poetry afficionados, tries to keep busy writing prose. She hopes you buy this book if only to save future generations from her poems.

<u>The Underpass</u>

Nadine prodded Marky's thigh with the toe of her grubby white boot to check he wasn't dead. She often found him like that, sprawled out from under his cardboard cover, his mouth gaping open. She liked to waken him up, welcome him into his hangover and drag him from the underpass to Mags' caff for beans on toast and a hot coffee bought with her overnight earnings.

Marky grunted and turned on his side, pulling the unfolded cardboard box with him. A corner of it was blackened and curled upwards. She grabbed at it and burnt flakes fell to the pavement beside a cigarette end.

'Good grief,' she said, grabbing at his shoulder, 'somebody's nearly turned you into a roast dinner.'

Marky jolted awake and frowned at her, his heavy dark eyebrows furrowed. He brushed his unruly, curly hair back with a beefy hand.

'What're you on about, woman?' he said grumpily.

Nadine pulled the burnt corner under his nose.

'That's what I'm on about, Marky. Someone's dropped a fag on you in the night and you were too pissed to even notice.'

She threw the cardboard down in disgust and looked back along the underpass, as though expecting to see the perpetrator peering at her from the foot of the steps.

She had to tell him again when they were in the caff, facing each other over the formica table, Nadine with a cup of Mags' strong black tea, Marky with his beans.

'You can't stay there any more,' she said, tugging a pile of scratchcards from her pocket and handing half of them to him, 'it doesn't matter if it was an accident or not. One way or another sleeping out'll be the end of you.'

'And what you do at night is safe I suppose?'

Marky gave her one of his looks and then took one of the cards and started rubbing automatically at the gilt boxes.

'Anyway, where else am I going to go,' he said, shaking his head, 'maybe I should just get myself banged up again?'

'You could go to the men's hostel,' she said, screwing up another card and adding it to the growing pile in the centre of the table. She wished their lives were more normal and then she and Marky could be boyfriend and girlfriend instead of just company for breakfast.

'You need to be somewhere you can sleep without having to get boozed up. What about the place on Kendrick Way?'

He shrugged, 'I don't mind going there in the day for a wash but I'm not staying there at night. They're all barking. They'd have a knife in me for looking at them the wrong way. You should know what that's like.'

He looked at her pointedly and Nadine looked away. She didn't want to be reminded of Danny.

'Last one,' she said, holding the card up ceremoniously, 'Cool Cash, you have to find a temperature lower than the one on the card but you can only scrape one box.'

'What's the temperature on the card?'

'Seven.'

'Seven what?'

'I don't know,' she said, impatiently rubbing at the box beneath, 'damn, it's a nine. I should have got you to choose, for luck.' She gathered the crumpled cards up and dropped them into her empty cup.

She left Marky in the café with a second cup of coffee and made her way back to the refuge to get Sam up for school. When she got to their room she found a folded piece of paper under the door and scanned her eyes over it.

'It has been brought to our notice that you persist in leaving your thirteen year old son alone in your room at night. We are not here to judge how you spend your time but the neglect of your son will not be tolerated while you are under our roof.'

She cast her eyes to the bottom of the letter.

'This is your third and final warning. You have seven days to find alternative accommodation. Please note that your social worker Jasmine Williams will be here at 10.00 to discuss your options.'

She dropped it into the bin and prodded Sam awake, 'you alright, hon,' she asked him, 'I've got you a bacon sandwich and some juice.'

By quarter to ten Nadine was downstairs in the communal lounge in a pair of jeans and jumper, her fair hair clean and scraped back in a pony tail. She'd washed in stone cold water, on purpose, but she was still having trouble staying awake. She went outside for a cigarette and was leaning against the wall when the social worker arrived.

'I can't believe you're still on the game,' was Jasmine's opening shot, as Nadine stubbed her cigarette out on the pavement, 'you told me you only did it because Danny made you but they tell me here you're out nearly every night.'

'Where else will I get money?' Nadine heard the whine in her voice but couldn't help it, as she followed Jasmine through reception to the lounge, 'I've got to buy stuff for Sam.'

'We worked out a perfectly good budget for you on your benefits,' Jasmine was pulling a file out of her bag, 'if you didn't waste so much on scratchcards and gave up smoking you'd be a lot better off.'

Nadine sat down and curled her legs under her. Her early meetings with Jasmine had been quite different. Then she had been all tea and sympathy.

'I need a bit of a life,' she said.

'So does Sam,' was Jasmine's response and Nadine shifted in her chair.

'The only option I've got for you is bed and breakfast over in Newham and that really is your last chance. If you blow that then it's fostering for Sam and you'll be listed as voluntarily homeless. I can't do anything else for you if you won't help yourself.'

Nadine wanted to get angry but she knew there was no point. It was Jasmine that had got them away from Danny, coming round in her own car at four in the morning, after she'd phoned her. She knew Jasmine had got into trouble for giving a client her own number but that was her all over. She wasn't one for minding her own business. Jasmine left her with a leaflet, '*Getting Yourself off the Street*', Nadine dropped it straight in the bin. It was just until one of the scratchcards came up trumps.

That night Nadine tried not to think about what she was doing as she got dressed in her short skirt and plunging top. She wished she had Jasmine's warm coat, it looked like it might dip below freezing tonight. She looked back at Sam, lying asleep in his bed. They were already chucking her out. Another night or two wouldn't make any difference now.

Nadine kept away from the busier streets. She didn't want to get mixed up with the competition with no-one to protect her. At least Danny had made sure no-one lamped her. She'd hang back in the shop doorways until she saw someone driving slowly, keeping an eye out along the pavement. Then she'd step forward and show herself. She was always careful not to say anything until they did, that way you didn't make mistakes, didn't end up in a cell for the night.

There didn't seem to be anyone about. After midnight she moved nearer to the underpass. She was worried about Marky and it would be a bit warmer to take the punter down the steps. About one in the morning an old cavalier drew up with one purple wing. A middle aged man with a crew cut nodded at her. She nodded back.

He got out of the car. She stepped forward one step and nodded towards the underpass steps.

'Twenty,' he said. It wasn't much and she hesitated while she thought about it.

'Just oral,' he grunted.

He refused to hand over the money until they were at the bottom of the steps and then shoved a note in her hand. She turned to go back to the streetlamp to check it and tuck it in her boot but he caught her arm.

'I can't see what it is,' she said.

'It's a twenty,' he replied, pulling her back with a too strong grip on her arm.

She wrenched her arm free and held the note back towards

the top of the steps, 'it looks like a fiver to me,' she said, squinting in the low light. The man grabbed her round the waist and pulled her against the wall.

'It's what you're worth so just get on with it,' he said forcing her head down with one hand clenched around her hair. She gasped but tried to keep calm. Turning on the charm usually worked at least for a few minutes. She needed that time to work out what to do. Sometimes it was best to just cut your losses and do what they wanted.

'Let me up a minute,' she wheedled, 'at least let me get comfortable.'

She twisted her head round towards where she could just see Marky's outline under his cardboard cover. The man was still holding Nadine's hair in a tight grip while forcing his zip down with his other hand. Then he reached into his pocket and pulled out a flick knife.

'Do it, you little whore.'

She tried not to gasp but let him push her until she was level with his groin. Then she forced her head forward with all her strength, butting him where it would hurt most. He shouted out in agony and released his grip. She pulled her head back out of range of the knife and ran in the opposite direction into the underpass, towards Marky. Throwing herself down beside him she pulled at his shoulders. There was an overpowering smell of super strength lager.

The man was straightening up by the steps but there was no sign of Marky wakening. She shook him more violently and shouted in his ear. The man had started to come along the passage. She could see the silouhette of the knife against the opening behind him. He was staggering slightly, holding himself up with one hand padding along the wall.

'I'll take you and your friend too you little bitch.'

She crouched down, helpless, beside Marky's inert body as
the man drew nearer. She thought of Sam. What a mess
she'd made of his life. What kind of life was she giving him?

Suddenly she had an idea. She pulled the cardboard sheets
towards her rolling them up quickly into a column and
reached for her lighter. The cardboard was slightly damp
and didn't catch right away. She tried the other end. A trail
of smoke first and then an orange glow and then it was
alight. She stood up and held the burning roll of cardboard in
front of her, jabbing it at the man.

'You fucking witch,' he exclaimed,'you're mad.' He leant
against the wall. She lunged towards him. The flames
brushed at his chest. She smelt singeing wool.

'Jesus,' he said, 'you're schizo.' She pulled back and then she
swept her home made flame thrower from side to side
screaming out all the anger and hurt that she'd carried in her
for years.

She didn't see him turn and run. She didn't hear Marky get
up and walk over to her pulling the remains of the burning
cardboard out of her hands before she hurt herself. She just
collapsed crying into his arms.

It was too smoky to stay in the underpass. They came up to
ground level and without making any plan ended up at the
caff, curling up together in the doorway and waiting for the
dawn.

'You can't do that anymore,' Marky said, running his finger
under her eyes, scooping up her tears, 'we'll find some way
out of this together.'

Mags found them sleeping there when she came to open up

and nudged them awake, insisting they come in and get warm.

'You two are my most regular customers,' she said, pulling a chair out for Nadine and then putting her own coat around her shoulders, 'I'll get the heating on.'

'I've only got a fiver,' Nadine told her when she got back, 'I need to get something for Marky and to take back to Sam. I don't need anything for me.'

'Rubbish,' Mags said moving behind the door to fetch her overall, 'what would you like, on the house, you can pay me back another day.'

Nadine began to cry again.

'Where's my hankies,' Mags said reaching into the pocket of her overall and pulling out a packet of tissues, 'here you are.'

A small rectangle of card fell onto the floor.

'You dropped something,' Marky said, picking it up. He smoothed it out on the table. It was the Cool Cash scratch-card from the previous morning.

'Didn't I bin that?' Nadine asked, rubbing at her nose with a tissue.

'Oh, yes,' Mags answered her, 'when I was throwing them out I thought you'd missed out, because there were some unscratched foil bits, but then I saw you only got one go. I meant to drop it in the bin.'

Marky was looking down at it, puzzled, 'You have to get a lower temperature than the one they give you right?'

Nadine nodded, 'They've got seven, we've got nine so we lost.'

Marky shook his head, 'No, they've got minus seven and we've got minus nine.'

'So?' Nadine couldn't see any difference.

'So you've won ten grand!'

Nadine snatched the card from him and stared at it.

'I could buy a car,' she said, 'or a holiday in America, Disneyland' her eyes shone.

Marky put his hand over the ticket, 'or you could pay the deposit and rent on a flat, buy a suit for job interviews, learn a skill and then you could save up for those things. You need to give up what you've been doing. You need a fresh start.'

Nadine looked into Marky's face smiling at her good fortune. She would speak to Jasmine about this. Get her to help her find a nice little flat near Sam's school, help her work out a budget to make it last till she could get a job. Jasmine was always on about getting her some retraining. Nadine put her hand over Marky's. He could have kept quiet and just slipped the card into his pocket. That's what Danny would have done.

'I will if you will,' she said tapping the back of his fingers, 'I will if you will.'

Joe Ridgwell

Joe has been widely published on the underground scene and descriptions of him range from 'the hard man of British writing', 'a talented sonofabitch', to a 'literary thug genius'. He thinks we are seeing the decline of western civilization and relishes the prospect of imminent doom. Fight fire with fire, he says, keep searching for the lost elation and load the literary guns!

Portrait of the Artist as a Young Man

After three weeks living in a local YMCA the authorities handed L-Boy a grotty bed-sit at the bottom of the high street, the shitty rat infested end. That's all the council could come up with after his mum chucked him out for pissing in the washing machine. It was the final straw, she said. Shortly afterwards I bumped into him outside the job centre.

'Wanna see me new pad?'

'Ok,' I said.

L-Boy's new pad was situated above a row of grubby Asian-owned premises, sari shops, newsagents, tailors, etc. The first thing I noticed was the battered aluminium door. The second thing I noticed was the smell, an almost overpowering wave of curry assaulting my nostrils.

I held a jumper sleeve to my nose to deflect the potent aromas. L-Boy lived on the fourth floor and on the way up we passed a cramped communal kitchen. Inside several women were busy at work, stirring pots, chopping vegetables, all the while keeping up a stream of cacophonous Bengali.

'Rinky dinks in ere dunnit?' I said.

'Full on,' said L-Boy.

It was dark inside the room and smelled of unwashed bed linen, dirty socks and stale curry. A spunk-stained single mattress and an ancient looking dresser dominated the room. A grey sheet hung across the only window shut out any hint of natural daylight and in one corner a few porno mags lay here and there.

I sat down next to the bed, grabbed a wank mag and casually flicked the pages.

'Ow's it going?' I asked, as I viewed a pair of huge breasts.

'Sweet as bruv, bout time you moved out as well ain't it?'

I gave the dismal surroundings a cursory once over, 'yeah mate, whatever.'

L-Boy lit up a fag, Lambert & Butler, 'I can do what I fucking want these days. No nagging old woman, no pissed-up fucking stepdad on me case every five seconds.'

'So what ya saying geez?'

'Freedom bruv, that's what I'm saying.'

I had to admit L-Boy had a point, 'yeah, freedom, I could do with some of that, but this place is a dump.'

L-Boy pulled a face, 'it's all the fucking council would give me, but it's only temporary. In a few weeks I should get me own gaff; toilet, bathroom, kitchen, all mod-con's.'

'Sweet,' I replied without averting my gaze from the bird in the magazine, a blonde sort who was taking one in the pink and one in the stink, 'ave ya found a job yet?'

L-Boy stood up and walked over to the window, 'na, but I've got a few things lined up.'

'Such as?'

'This and that.'

Basically fuck all then, but I said nothing.

I pushed aside the sheet and peered at the dirty street.

'Game of pool in the Horse and Cart?'

'Let's go.'

Aside from one barmaid, four burnt-out old geezers, and a
mad woman, the pub was empty. I ordered a couple of wife
beaters, while L-Boy racked em up. He broke with consum-
mate skill and three yellows went in off.

'Jammy fucker.'

L-Boy chalked his cue and smiled smugly. Then he manoeu-
vred swiftly into an angled cuing position.

'Check this out.'

I checked it out, another yellow to the top corner.
Bollocks. Four shots later it was all over.

'Whitewash.'

I swigged my beer and retreated to the bar. L-Boy had been
playing pool ever since he was big enough to see over a table,
so fucked if I was ganna waste another squid trying to even
up the scores. We sat and drunk our beers in silence. Then
we went outside and smoked a cigarette each. Outside the
world was still in motion, people going here and there, doing
whatever it is people with a purpose do.

At five a group of road workers entered the boozer. After getting in drinks they headed straight to the pool table. I
watched as L-Boy strolled over and placed a pound coin on
the table. The road workers were all big lumps and a few
stares were issued.

'Winner stays on,' mumbled L-Boy in his shaky falsetto.

'Yeah alright mate,' replied a gruff voice.

Half an hour later L-Boy was at the table and holding court.

He won the first game narrowly, lost the second easily, and then laid down the challenge,

'Fiver a game?' He offered.

Encouraged by L-Boy's less than adroit cuing skills and two pints of wife beater each, the roadies fell for the bait hook line and sinker.

After those deceptive preliminaries L-Boy took no prisoners and was as ruthless as fuck. Some games later the road workers had been massacred. I gave them a cursory glance, checking for signs of retribution, but they seemed to take the humiliation in good spirits, and quickly moved on to an electronic quiz machine.

L-Boy strolled over like Charlie Big Bananas.

'What a bunch of mugs, total wipe-out.'

'Ow much you up?'

'Fifty boys.'

'Your round then ain't it?'

'Wife beater?'

I nodded.

An hour later we stumbled out of the pub and headed straight to the nearest chippie. L-Boy was falling over drunk. The takeaway was empty aside from one guy in a leather jacket. L-Boy stumbled through the doorway and eyeballed the stranger.

'Fuck me, its Bob Biscuit in his leather jacket.'

The man glanced up from eating a huge donner kebab, 'What you say?' He asked in foreign-sounding accent.

L-Boy went to tell him, but I quickly clamped a hand over his mouth and bundled him towards the counter.

'Sorry mate he's a bit pissed, been celebrating his birthday an that.'

The man grumbled something unintelligible and recommenced chomping on his greasy kebab.

'Wha you wan?' Asked the Chinese fish and chip shop owner.

L-Boy gazed at what was on offer and then.

'Large chip roll, two pickled eggs, sausage in batter, pickled onion, gherkin, one savaloy, and er, yeah, a fish cake.'

The Chinese man didn't bat an eyelid and once L-Boy was served I ordered an extra large shish. While we waited for the kebab L-Boy stood there wobbling and leering at the man in the leather jacket. Fortunately the man appeared to pay zero attention, but just as we went to leave, L-Boy felt it appropriate to lob a pickled onion over his shoulder. The onion landed in the astonished man's lap.

I glanced at L-Boy.

'Toes it!' We yelled in near unison.

We ran full pelt along the high street, took a short-cut through a small council estate, and then ducked back along a hidden alley.

'You cunt,' I gasped, as soon as we'd lost Bob Biscuit.

L-Boy stopped running and stared glumly at his wrappers.

Then he pulled out one forlorn looking pickled egg.

'Fucking 'ell, lost all me munch.'

I pulled out my kebab and stuffed half a pitta into me gob.

'Good, serves ya right.'

'Give us some?' moaned L-Boy.

'Fuck off,' I mumbled between bites.

After that we bought ten cans of strong polish beer at the twenty four hour shop and went straight back to L-Boy's. When we got there we found, much to our surprise, his fifteen year-old step sister Sonia. She was holding a black plastic bag,

'Where you been?' She demanded.

L-Boy blinked and bobbed his head like an old chicken.

'What the fuck youse doing ere?'

'Been chucked out as well 'en I?'

'So what?'

'So, thought I could crash round yours.'

After the sixth attempt L-Boy slipped the key in the lock.

'Ten pounds a night lady.'

Sonia nudged me, 'Even charge his own sister, the tight arse.'

I laughed, 'And wait till ya see the state of the place.'

Once inside the room we sat around drinking the tins. I was sat next to Sonia and with the beer goggles on she was starting to look like a serious sort. Three cans in I decided I wanted to see what she looked like in the buff.

'What about a game of strip poker?' I offered into the fetid air.

By this stage L-Boy was well gone. He raised his can, 'Yeah bruv.'

I glanced at Sonia, 'Youse up for it?' I asked.

Sonia crossed her legs and took a defiant swig from her can of lager, 'Fuck yeah.'

I pulled out the deck of cards I kept on my person at all times.

'I'll be dealer.'

'Ow comes you're dealer?' Queried Sonia.

I flashed a cheeky wink and nodded towards her brother, 'Twenty ones yeah?'

Sonia nodded and L-Boy raised his can again, 'Yeah bruv.'

Five deals later Sonia was down to bra and knickers and, aside from a manky pillow hiding his crown jewels, L-Boy was stark bollock naked. As for me I was down to me Levi's, but only so as not to arouse any suspicions. I shuffled the cards once more, making sure I'd be certain to get ace/king.

'What ya got L?' I asked.

L-Boy raised his hand and screwed up his eyes. Then he leered at Sonia for ages, before trying to grab one of her tits in a weird slow-motion action.

Sonia eyeballed her brother's drunken lunge, screamed, lobbed her can into the air and jumped into my arms. Being no mug I grabbed her tight.

'Shit, did ya see that? Me own bruv trying to grab me?'

I nodded and then we both looked in L-Boy's direction. His pillow had gone flying and he'd fallen back on the bed. He was spark out, but somehow possessed a massive boner.

'Oh my god, ya see that thing, what a dirty fucker,' gasped Sonia.

I run a hand inside one of Sonia's bare thighs.

'L-Boy what the fuck is that shit?'

L-Boy grunted, spluttered and then turned onto his stomach.

'Geezer's fucked,' I said.

Sonia put one arm around my neck and stuck a hand on my crotch.

'Let's fuck.'

Seconds later I was lying on top of L-Boy's step-sister, poling the arse off it, all the while keeping one beady eye on him just in case he woke up and gave me grief. Sonia had her legs wide open and was taking all I had.

'Don't come inside, don't fucking come inside me,' she kept whispering lustfully into my ear.

Fuck that shit. Last thing I needed was to get that divvy tart in the club, but strangely when the time came I forgot to pull out and spurted my load right up her.

'You bastard,' gasped Sonia.

***

I awoke in the early morning to the potent whiff of curry, which made me gag. L-Boy was fast asleep, snoring fitfully, and Sonia was clinging to my body like some unwelcome human limpet. Taking great care and caution I slowly un-peeled her arms and legs and then stumbled into a corner and puked quietly all over L-Boy's porno collection.

Surprisingly neither of them roused so I slipped sheepishly down the creaky staircase and out into another shit rain-piss day.

Touch.

Danny King

Danny is the author of eight books and the smash-hit BBC3 comedy, 'Thieves Like Us' (anyone see it? No, us neither). Having just turned forty he genuinely thinks things were better in the Eighties when people only dropped litter on the floor because all the bins had been removed following a prolonged IRA bombing campaign. Go find him at www.dannykingbooks.com.

The Sleep Walker

Richard was cold and he didn't know why. His bare skin was pockmarked with goose bumps and his ears numb with chill. On looking around the room he realised the reason for his discomfort; his blankets had floated up off his bed and were now stuck to the ceiling.

He climbed out of bed to pull them back down but they were too high. He stood on the mattress but still they were out of his reach. He stacked chairs on tables on boxes on crates, but still his blankets were beyond his grasp.

It was then that Richard noticed all his windows were open, allowing in the cold night air. A chill wind began to blow through the gaping openings and envelope Richard with icy fingers.

He was cold. So cold.

Why hadn't he noticed his windows were open when he went to bed? He went to close them, but couldn't. They too were beyond his reach. In fact they were right the way across the room, across the street, across the town, and every step he took towards them just drove them further and further away. His legs felt like lead as he struggled headfirst into what felt like a force ten gale, desperately reaching for the latches.

But it was no use. So cold. So very cold.

He lifted his eyes and all but broke down with despair when he saw, far far away, almost beyond the distant horizon, his windows rattling and crashing about loose in the storm. He managed only one or two more hard-fought steps towards them before finally they slipped out of sight.

It was bitter. He'd never known anything like it. His bones ached and his skin burned with the cold.

He had to get those blankets. He had no choice now. He looked around and saw that the wind had dislodged them from the ceiling and they were now caught in the branches of a tree. They whipped about in the squall and threatened to blow away at any second, but for the moment they were caught.

Again he tried to reach them, but they were still just beyond his grasp. What's more, the wind was now plucking them from the tree, twig by twig, and threatening to deprive Richard of his last hope of warmth. He couldn't let that happen. He'd die from the cold if it did. He had to get those blankets.

Coiling himself up like a jack-in-the-box, he leapt skyward in one last attempt to snatch his bedclothes from the tree - but once again, he missed.When he landed, it wasn't on the thick shag pile carpet his feet had left a second earlier, but on concrete. His knees buckled underneath his weight and Richard crumpled to the ground in a heap. His hands, arms, knees and legs scuffed on the cold, hard pavement and he winced with both pain and shock.

This, however, paled into consideration next to the shock he got when reality flooded back to his senses and he suddenly saw where he was.

The street was quiet. No lights or signs of life came from any of the houses and there was no traffic on the road. Richard stood up, keeping to the shadows in order to shield his naked body from the orange street lighting.

He shivered uncontrollably, not least of all because of the cold, which was now much more apparent and intense in reality than had been in his dream.

He guessed by the darkness that it must be around three or four o'clock, though with the angry black clouds low in the night's sky, almost ready to unleash their burden upon the sleeping town, it could also have been a lot later. He had to get home.

He recognised the street in which he found himself immediately. It was the main street down to the railway station. He knew this primarily because he walked it every morning as part of his journey to work, but also because he had woken up in it twice already this month.

The first time, the shock had nearly killed him. All he remembered of the previous evening was a late one at the office, fish & chips from the take-away and two or so hours of telly before turning in. His bed had been soft and inviting that night and he had welcomed the first waves of sleep as they washed over his consciousness.

A terrifying, cold, hard confusion greeted Richard the next time he had opened his eyes, ripping him from the warmth and security he'd known only moments earlier and tossing him screaming into the street. Only ten or twelve doors up from his house, he had found his way home quickly and easily enough, but struggled to understand what had happened to him as he revived himself in front of his two-bar fire. He convinced himself in his delirium that he had been abducted by aliens or drugged and left for dead, or something equally nasty. But he revised this theory a couple of nights later when he once again found himself in the street.

This time, he had sought the assistance of a passer-by, a funky young clubber who looked like she was on her way back from a night out.

'Help, help me,' he had called to her. 'Please I'm not a pervert, I just think I'm going mad. Help me please, help me.'

Hindsight is a wonderful thing and half an hour later, kneeling in front of his fire, he couldn't blame the young girl for screaming at the sight of him and fleeing for her life. In fact, he'd done much the same thing a split-second later, trusting his own feet over the judgement of others.

He started to shake uncontrollably now as he hopped and skipped over the rough tarmac, darting from parked car to bush to post box to tree, hand on his privates, heart in his mouth, frantic to get back to the sanctuary of his house, now just three streets away.

When he paused at the street corner and peered around a bush, he almost burst a blood vessel when he saw a police car heading his way, now no more than fifty yards away.

He stared at it helplessly, momentarily frozen to the spot with indecision and panic, before finally launching himself headfirst over the nearest fence.

The car seemed to slow as it passed, fuelling the paranoia in Richard's mind, that the policemen inside had chosen this particular fence to check behind tonight in their relentless search for sexual deviants.

How could he explain this? He'd try, of course, but in their shoes, would he believe himself?

'I don't know what I'm doing out here and naked. I must have been sleep-walking.'

'But we have a report of a naked man fitting your description accosting a young lady only last week. She claims that the man spoke to her and was fully lucid, if a little deranged.'

'Ah yes, but I'd woken up by then and just wanted her to help me.'

'Help you with what?'

He'd get three years for sure.

The panda moved off and Richard let out a croak of relief. This however, proved a little premature as the porch of the house, whose garden he was currently crouching in, suddenly exploded with light, sending a brilliant white glare across the lawn and across Richard's now blue skin.

'Who's out there?' demanded the angry voice, as the front door was wrenched open.

'What are you doing in my garden?'

Richard no longer cared if he was seen or not, as evasion now became the order of the day. Leaping back across the fence and into the street, he sprinted the rest of the way home and up the stairs to his bedroom, pausing only briefly to smash his way in through the downstairs hallway window - for the third time this month.

The next day, Richard bought a pair of pyjamas and some thick woollen night socks.

As a child Richard had suffered horribly from night time wanderings. He remembered waking the whole neighbour- hood up with his terrified screams and helpless wails. He remembered the thrashing of his heart and the uncontrol- lable terror at finding himself far from the comfort and safety of home and at the mercy of the black, hungry shadows. He'd woken up in forests and fields, garages and gardens, cul-de- sacs and crescents. Once, he'd even woken up in the back of a builder's van. The builder was halfway to work before discov- ering the screaming child and had one hell of a job trying to explain the situation to a vigilant roadside police officer and an ever growing angry lynch mob.

But that was twenty-five years ago.A distant memory from a long forgotten childhood. How could it be happening again?

From now on, Richard decided, he would go to bed with a front door key on a chain around his neck and a tenner for a taxi. The best plan though, would be to ensure he didn't leave the house in the first place.

One solution, Richard thought, would be to get into the habit of putting the front door latch on before he went to bed. But a short cab ride home from Milton Crescent three nights later proved that this idea was fatally flawed. Dead locks too seemed no deterrent. If he could make it three quarters of the way to the station in his sleep, then a few locks, bolts and latches had little dissuasive power.

He even tried hiding the dead lock key from himself just before he went to bed, but his nocturnal nomadic self would always know where to find it. The price of living by oneself, Richard thought.

In one final desperate resort, Richard visited a sex shop in the city and bought himself a pair of handcuffs. And that night, he chained his wrist to the iron-wrought bedstead, threw the key beyond his reach and drifted off to sleep.

***

The last trains of the night had ushered through the station just before midnight and now the ticket office and machines were shut up and silent. The only sounds to be heard on this dark and blustery morning were the howling wind, as it rattled though the platform guttering, and the incessant ticking of the station clock.

It was a little after two when Richard arrived, sauntering silently in his thick woollen night socks and carrying his bedstead as if it were his briefcase.

Eyes closed and otherwise lifeless, he took his place on the platform just a couple of feet from the edge and in-between the elderly Quantity Surveyor in the red silk pyjamas and the naked Secretarial Assistant. No one looked at each other. No one stared. These nightly commuters merely dreamed.

All along both platforms, north bound and south, they stood in night shirts, dressing gowns, bedclothes and bare, waiting like the ranks of the undead, their numbers steadily growing as the night rolled on.

The gale continued to blow, swirling hair across faces and riding night dresses up bodies, carrying droplets of rain from the low clouds that hung in the dark morning's sky. Still the passengers remained unmoved; unmoved that is until the stroke of three, when the train pulled into the station and stopped near perfectly at the six carriage halt. It's driver adorned in blue cotton pyjama bottoms, opened the automatic doors and silently Richard and the others filed on board and took their seats.

Once his passengers were all safely ensconced, the driver closed the doors and engaged the accelerator. And slowly, but surely, the train pulled away from the station and headed into the night.

<u>Roz Southey</u>

Roz is a novelist living in the North-East of England. Her short stories have appeared in a number of small press magazines and her first novel, a historical crime caper named 'Broken Harmony' was published in April '07; a follow-on, 'Chords and Discords' appeared in July '08 and the third in the series will appear in May '09. Jesus, she's too good for us...!

Another Life

I'd always known it was either me or Keeg. Mates then ene-
mies. One of us was going to have to die.

It was never fucking well going to be me.

***

The flat is dark, full of shadows. As I walk naked across the
room, moonlight stripes the floor. The polished wood, paid
for with my hard-earned. Floor to ceiling windows, velvet
curtains. Chrome and glass furniture, plasma screen tv, pictures worth a fortune. We used to look up at blocks like this,
me and Keeg, back when we were fourteen. Poncy fuckers,
we'd yell. Fucking fat-cats. And pudgy-faced wankers in
posh suits would peer out at us in a mixture of fury and fear.

Now I'm the one looking out.

Down below, in the courtyard, there are four yobs, toting
beer cans, shadowboxing. Keeg's there, doubling up in mock
agony at a play kick to his guts. One of the yobs lumbers
over to an ornamental tree, hikes down his zip and pisses.
My mates. Twenty somethings who still think like fourteen
year olds. Who spend their lives stoned out of their minds.
Drink or drugs, who cares. We started with glue nicked from
Woolies then bought E on street corners and moved on to the
hard stuff. Okay, so I have that kind of stuff now, stashed at
the bottom of the biscuit tin. But I earned the cash to buy it
with; Keeg and his mates just pinched something.

Keeg's shouting up at me. He sees me. Our eyes meet. And
hate. He hates me for going over to the other side. I hate
him for reminding me what I once was.

I let the blind snap back into place. How the hell did they get
through the security gate? You have to show the guard your

ID, look into a camera, that sort of shit. And why are they here, anyway? To piss me off, that's why.

There were five of us and me and Keeg were top dogs. Kev and Keegan - unbelievable - we thought it was meant. We bossed the gang, we said what fucking went and we fucking did it. Go to school? What the fuck do you learn at school? You've got to be out there, grabbing the world by the balls and letting it know what's what. Want some money? Take it. Want some drink? Steal it.

We lived it up like crazy. We had the entire neighbourhood shitting its pants when they saw us. Standing outside the supermarket with our hoods up, kicking at the walls, leering at the kids in their prams, running straight at the oldies, swerving only at the last moment so they'd totter and shout.

Christ, it was good.

Except.

Except for those lousy evenings when it was pissing it down and no one would let us in the pubs and even the students in Kentucky Fried Chicken chased us out. Bizzy cars cruised past, winding their windows down and the pigs taking a good long insolent look at us. Those were the nights we'd break windows, to hear the glass break and alarm bells howl. The nights we wondered what the fuck we were doing here, what the world was all about and who cared anyway. Bored as hell.

I dress. Jeans, t-shirt, leather jacket, trainers. Only the best. The guy who stares back at me from the mirror looks good. Good face, good body. Not your average wanker. And all the clothes're top quality, none of your mass-produced shit. I've left all that behind. Way behind. Only the best. Particularly when you're going out to kill.

First time we did it, we were scruffy. Worse than scruffy, we looked shite. Keeg's t-shirt had more holes than shirt, I'd spilt beer down my hoodie, hell, I'd been sick down it. And my jeans. Frayed to start with and I wore them right down on my hips so I could get the crotch real low. Keeg said they made me waddle and he could see my underpants and they weren't clean. Not pretty at all.

He was a kid, the one we found. Homeless. Huddled in a doorway, with big eyes full of tears and a nose dripping snot. Eighteen maybe. We were fourteen. And there were five of us - that made up for him being bigger than us.

'Hey, mate,' Keeg said, 'want some beer?' He held out the half-full can, the kid grabbed for it. Keeg upended the can and poured it over his head.

The kid went mental. He screamed and shouted and kicked out with his feet and flailed around with his arms. One of his feet caught Keeg on the shin and he swore.

'Fucking fucking fucking shit,' he yelled. 'What the fuck are you doing?' And he kicked back.

Then we were all doing it. Kicking and stamping and jump- ing up and down and hearing cloth tear and bone crack. And I stomped, and went on stomping, and on and on until there was only blood and the shrieks subsided into groans. All the anger went into my feet and came out again with every jump and in the end there was nothing left except the kind of relieved emptiness you get after wanking.

And you know why we didn't get caught? Some fucker had smashed the CCTV. We washed off the blood in puddles, then lit a bonfire under our clothes in one of the sheds on the allotments and burnt the whole place down. Vandalism, they called it. Fucking coppers didn't have a clue.

The next one, me and Keeg did on our own. This time we
went looking. Maybe three weeks later. Fucking truant officer had been round and my mum's boyfriend gave me a beating for skipping school. As if he'd never done it when he was
a kid. Doesn't like me around all day, that's it, not since I
walked in on him and mum fucking on the settee. Christ,
that was horrible.

So we were out in the frost and the hail and it was a Monday
night in November and we'd already been thrown out of
three pubs for being too young. We'd tried nicking beer from
the off-licence but they'd run us off. So we pissed around the
city centre, getting stared at by bouncers and sniggered at by
girls wearing damn all.

'Hey,' Keeg said to one of them, 'fancy a bit of something,
then?'

She was twice his height and six times his weight and I bet
she'd never pulled a bloke in her life. But she just looked
down her nose at Keeg and said, 'I bet your willy's no bigger
than my kid sister's pinkie.'

Keeg went for her.

She screeched and kicked out and grabbed at his hair. His
head smashed into her boobs and she bullied him back
against the shop window, then kneed him in the groin. Then
she marched off with a sneer and a swagger.

'Bitch,' Keeg spluttered.

So we went looking for someone to kill. Keeg was raging.
'I'll find a bitch somewhere and fuck her and fuck her and
then I'll slice her tits off and fry them up for my supper.'

'Yeah, yeah,' I said not believing him.

'I will. I fucking will.'

We found someone at last, an elderly bloke by a cashpoint, peering with rheumy eyes at the huge letters and trying to fit his card into the slot with a shaking hand. We leapt on him from behind and he threw up his hands and went down at once with a great gusting sigh that scared the shit out of us. And then he lay still and never moved again.

'What kind of fucking fun was that?' Keeg said. So we went and killed a dog as well. And that wasn't much fun either.

I reckon we killed four maybe five people all told. I don't remember exactly. We were stoned half the time, or pissed. No one ever got near us, not cops, not neighbours. I remember me mam saying once how dirty my jeans were - we'd had to roll around in the mud with this wino before we could finish him off. Accidental death, they said that one was - fell in the river and drowned. Anyway, it was only a tramp - who cares about them?

But somewhere along the line I stopped enjoying it. There wasn't any anger left to come out. Or maybe it got changed into fear and that was scary in itself. I kept thinking it couldn't last. The cops aren't stupid. They'd catch us. Maybe they were onto us already and we just didn't know it. Then we'd spend the rest of our lives in jail and everyone would forget about us. There'd be nothing to do except kick the shit out of the walls.

I got stressed out about it. I kept looking over my shoulder. Every time a bizzy car went past, I thought they were playing with us and would just drive round the corner and catch us.

So when Keeg said, 'Let's go get a wino,' only a couple of weeks after the old guy, I puked in the gutter.

'You're scared,' Keeg said.

'Don't talk crap.'

'You're shitting your pants.'

'It's that fucking burger,' I said, 'it's giving me the runs.'

'Fuck the burger,' Keeg said, 'let's go get some fun.'

'I'm going home. I'm sick.'

'Scaredy cat,' he said contemptuously.

'Fuck off.'

I went home. Keeg went off by himself but didn't find anyone. Later, he said it hadn't seemed right without me. Then
he broke his leg. Running to get out of the way of his old
man when he was beating up everyone in sight. Ended up in
hospital for a month. Like he said, it wasn't fun on my own.
So I got into the way of going to the library and mucking
around on the internet. Then mam threw out the boyfriend
cos he slapped her and we went off to live with her sister
down south. And that was that - I didn't see Keeg for ten
years.

It wasn't any better down south. No one in my new school
wanted to know me - I had a stupid accent and didn't know
anything. So I stopped going and went down the library to
surf the internet and then mam won a bit on the lottery and
gave me a games station.

And it took off from there really. All the games were stupid.
Fantasy stuff, dragons, and aliens and other dull shit. I reckoned I ought to make up my own games, based on what me
and Keeg had done.

You don't wanna hear all of this - the bits about how I got
myself sorted. I found this guy who taught me how to do the

computer stuff - he made me pay of course but it was worth it. Faggot. I went to school to keep everyone off my back, but I didn't do anything, I just kept scribbling away, planning the games. Okay, so the first game I made up was shite and anyone playing it would have known exactly what me and Keeg had done and we would have ended up behind bars for the rest of our natural, but the later stuff was better. Much better.

I got it made in the end. I got a job with this small firm, just three of us. Made a name for ourselves and pulled in a mint of money. That's how I'm here, in this flat, with all this cash, and these clothes, and girls queuing up for fucks. And Keeg's out there, swigging beer and still wearing a hoodie and trainers he bought years ago. Sod all in his pockets and he's probably fucking the barmaid in the pub. That's why he hates me.

I saw him last week. First time in ten years. In the street outside Smiths. Still the same Keeg, the same tatty jeans and holey t-shirt. He looked me up and down and laughed.

'Wanker,' he said.

'Yeah,' I said, 'well at least I'm not a loser.'

We stood toe to toe, face to face.

'I know stuff about you,' he said, softly, 'I know about homeless kids and winos, and old gits whose hearts go pop the first time you say boo. Don't you piss me off.'

'I know things about you too,' I said.

Maybe I've lost my accent a bit, being away. A huge grin cracked his face and he said in a prissy precious voice.

'Know things too? Can't speak proper any more, right?'

That got to me somehow. Like saying I wasn't real.

'Sod off,' I said.

He muscled in on me till we were nose to nose. I could feel his hard-on.

'This is my town,' he said, 'you sod off.' And he added, whispering, 'you were the one that chickened out, remember. You were the one who sicked his guts up rather than tackle a pansy pervert.'

'Sod off,' I said again and walked away.

And ever since, he and his mates - once my mates - have been prancing around outside my flat. Fuck knows how they found me. First couple of nights they tossed stones into the courtyard and against the wall of the flats. The security guard went out and yelled at them; minutes later a bizzy car cruised by. By then Keeg and his mates had gone.

But tonight they're in the courtyard and the guard's nowhere to be seen. Course, I could call the law, but if I did that, Keeg could land me in the shit. That's what he's betting on, that I won't dare do anything. Shop him and I shop myself. Of course someone else in the flats is probably calling the cops. That's why I'm going to have to sort it. Now.

Keeg doesn't stand a chance.

I take the lift down. From the glass doors in the foyer, I can see the security booth at the gate, which I couldn't see from above. I can see feet in polished black shoes, toes up on the floor. That takes care of what happened to the security guard, I guess.

They come for me the minute I walk out the door but Keeg roars at them; they give him sour looks but stop.

'Me and you,' I say, hands in the pockets of my leather jacket.

'Yeah,' he says, and the others jump on the low walls of the
ornamental flowerbeds and sit there, beer cans in hand, legs
swinging like they were at the football.

'Make it fast,' Keeg said, 'someone'll have called the cops.'

'Sure,' I say and swagger up to him. He stinks of beer and
piss and vomit and once I stank like that too. This is what I
left behind, this is what I could have been. And what's he
seeing? A smart guy, with looks and brains, the kid he once
was, who made it out of here and who got everything life has
to offer. And what do I feel?

Sick to the heart. It's all shit and show. Nothing but nothing.

Nothing like what Keeg and me had. Why am I here? Because
I left him behind. I walked out on him, and left him to the
shit and the crap and the boredom and the beer, and all the
rest of the nothing we had when we were kids. I let him
down. He was my mate and I walked out on him. He's shit
but I'm shit too, just shit covered with a fine coat and we
both know it.

We stand nose to nose, face to face, chest to chest and Keeg's
not the only one with a hard-on. And I'm thinking: this is it,
this is real. All that other shit is just pretend. The only difference is that it pays, and means you can stand up and say
look at me. I'm an executive with my own internet business.
I'm respectable.

Yeah. Right. I let him down and that makes me worse than
him. Ten times worse.

And that's the way it's going to stay. If I can't be better, I'll
be worse. No way he's going to get the drop on me. No way

he can take me down. And I slip the kitchen knife between
his ribs and he stares wide-eyed and gives an odd little gurgle
and slips down the length of me, like an old pair of jeans
shucking off. And then he's lying on the ground and there's a
smear of blood down my t-shirt.

Simple as that. No big deal. And you know - no fun at all.
It's all shite. But at least I don't feel guilty any more. What's
to feel guilty about? Keeg got left behind and I didn't. I look
at the three yobbos. They're still staring at Keeg's body with
the knife in it.

'So he got in and killed the guard,' I said, 'then he panicked
and did for himself. Right?'

They hop down from the walls, pause, nod. Then they're
sauntering away towards the gate as if nothing has happened. So long, Keeg. So long, mate. No offence, but you're
just history.

I bend to wipe the knife clean of my fingerprints and close
Keeg's hand around it.

And why didn't I get caught? Keeg took the cameras out of
course, when he did for the guard. Just like I knew he would.
So no one would see what happened. He knew tonight was
the night we sorted it.

***

In the dark room, the moon stripes the polished floorboards.
I look out of my window at the courtyard. Empty. Just a
new guard in the security cabin, a cat prowling round the
flowerbeds.

Empty.

I did what was necessary. It was always going to come down

to me and Keeg facing off. And there could be only one winner.

But that's the point. He's dead, just a pile of ashes scattered
for the dogs to crap on. And without him, I'm nothing. Just
another fucking bag of shite with nowhere to go. We were
two sides of one coin and I destroyed it.

In a way, he won.

I'm going to go get myself someone. A wino maybe or a Big
Issue seller, or a foreign student who doesn't know where the
hell he is. Someone to kill some time. Someone to kill.

Hey, Keeg, this one's for you.

* *E X T R A S* *

Interviews

Stories

Prizes

This Issue...

Sheila Quigley

'Black Betty'

The Radgepacket Tapes

Competition Time

Win a signed copy of one of Sheila's books

The Radgepacket Tapes

Have you ever had one of them days where you're just tripping over dead bodies at every turn and slipping and sliding in their blood? You know man, when the little town you live in has a slew of corpses appearing here, there and everywhere? A bit like Midsomer Murders meets Shameless kind of thing? Nah? No neither have we BUT...we know someone who has. Step forward Sheila Quigley, all star crime writer and inspiration to every scribbler born without a silver spoon in their mouth.

Alreet Sheila, what's happening with you these days then?

Quite a lot, nearly finished book number six, *'Thorn in My Side'*. Reckon another two weeks should see it off to agent. In the meantime, I did the Santa Stroll at Durham, pictures on my website and had a great time, all for the mayor of Durham's charity to raise money for the blind. Have a few talks around the area in the beginning of the year these dates can also be found on my site. If anyone is looking for a good time with lots of authors check out Crimefest Bristol.

You're well regarded as a crime fiction writer. Was it a conscious decision to go into that genre or did you find that you started writing and just got dragged in that direction naturally?

In my bottom drawer there are two novels, one a horror the other a saga. I know now they aren't good enough to be published, horror is what I wanted to write, my agent suggested crime and now I'm loving it.

As well as the novels have you written anything else we should looking out for?

In May there will be a short story crime collection out, there will be short stories from over twenty UK crime writers, it is for breast cancer, please keep a look out for it. The publishers are Creme de la Crime.The Seahills story is called *'Hungry Eyes'*.

Who or what would you say was responsible for motivating young Sheila to take up the pen initially?

Young Sheila! **(Good Answer - Ed)**

It's bloody hard work getting a publisher or even an acknowlegdement that they haven't just used your precious manuscript for bog paper these days - how did you manage it?

A hell of a lot of luck and a damn good agent.

What are you reading at the minute then (apart from Radgepacket obviously)?

'The Death Chamber' by Sarah Rayne. A fantastic writer, also one of my daughter Janine's favorites. Just finished one of Ken Mcoy's - *'Loser'* - another gritty writer and throughly enjoyed James Rollings *'The Judas Strain'*.

Do you have a schedule you stick to in terms of words per day or do you have 'creative' days and 'non-creative' (ie fuck it I'm off down the pub) days?

I start work as soon as I fall out of bed and work on and off until its time to climb back in again. Except when it's a lovely day and I jump in the car and explore our fantastic northern countryside, there's nowhere on earth like it.

What have you lashed all the millions on then - Crème de Menthe, Caviar or Faberge Eggs?

Between four children,nine grand children and the tax man there's not a lot left for me!

We have a number of literary heroes here at BB Towers - who would you say yours were and why?

Stephen King, a fantastic writer, in my humble opinion the best in the world.

Any advice you could give the millions of writers and authors out there who never get a sniff of publication?

Never ever give up. You must have a thick skin, this game is all about rejection, just keep on going, while there is something out there, there is always hope.

Ever considered getting involved in that jungle thing with Ant & Dec?

Are you fucking mad?

Do you follow the old adage of 'write what you know'?

Yes and no. It all depends on what you are writing about. Fantasy, horror it all takes a brilliant imagination. But in every genre you need to know about people if you can't write good, strong, interesting people then you might as well give up.

Who would play you in the film of your life?

Can't begin to imagine. She would of course have to be damn well stunning

And what sort of soundtrack would you like playing?

Living On A Prayer, which I did for more years than I care to remember.

Did you find that you had to change your style or content to get publishers interested in you initially?

After sending the horror and saga novels around and getting nowhere I decided to write a screenplay about ciggie smuggling in the North East. I sent it to Darley Anderson, who phoned me up the day that he got it and said brilliant but very hard to sell a screen play by an unknown, would I write a gangster novel set in the North East. Well that was it, I headed straight up stairs with a huge grin on my face and started '*Run for Home*'. The rest as they say is history. I was still in shock eight months later when a huge outdoor television camera rolled down the street and stopped at my door.

And the titles of your books being song titles - how did that happen?

Run for Home was actually playing on the radio that day and I thought it a great title and have followed through with song titles ever since, even the short story '*Hungry Eyes*' is a song title.

Does that lead to any copyright problems?

Song titles are not copyright.

And finally, but most importantly, assuming that your books become massive, multi million pound film productions is there any chance you might need a fifteen stone shaven headed Geordie to play a lead role and get all the girls??

One can always dream! **(she's not wrong - ED)**

The Radgepacket team and all at Byker Books would like to take this opportunity to thank Sheila for giving us her time so freely during this interview. We wish her continued success with her writing career and urge you all to check out her books.

We would also like to re-assure any concerned readers that despite the body count on show in her tales it's a bit like the A Team and no-one really dies...well unless they try to nick her Faberge Eggs - she chops their fucking hands off then like!

Black Betty

Staring out of the bus window Betty Wilkinson impatiently tapped her foot, the bus had been late again and would be even later dropping her at the stop she wanted the way this flaming slow coach was driving. The bloody Seahills, God she hated the place, everyone so friendly and so bloody nosy. You couldn't even fart in peace.

She nodded in the right places, not really listening to Doris Musgrove or Dolly Smith rabbiting on about poor Mr Skillings heart attack and if the old sod would make it out of hospital or not.

Like she gave a flying fuck?

The nine months she'd stood this place, was nine months too long.

Completely unaware that the neighbours she despised had given her the nickname Black Betty, mostly because she nearly always wore black as if she was for ever in mourning, but also because of her permanent scowl, she was thinking, time to go, time to leave this place behind. Every one was far too friendly, she didn't need their nosiness or their helpful-ness, didn't want it. God even most of the kids were helpful, and that friggin Lumsdon lot.

Her plans had been made for a while, they always were, she usually hung around a bit longer than this just to be on the safe side but claustrophobia was beginning to set in. If she heard one more good morning on a miserable rainy fucking day, she'd scream.

She caught sight of her reflection in the opposite window, she quite liked the new hair do and whatever chemicals and sprays the hairdresser had used made her dark hair really shine. She fastened the top button on her black coat, the nights had cut in and the clocks had just gone back, though not quite winter there was a definite nip in the air.

At last her stop appeared and she squeezed past the other passengers in a drastic hurry to escape her neighbours. Not caring that she stepped on an old woman's toes and nearly winded a teenager wearing a hoodie that was the same colour as her coat, as she elbowed herself past him and got off the bus. She noticed the poster outside of the paper shop simply because the wind had managed to loosen two corners, one at the top and one at the bottom, and the poster was flapping about every so often exposing the same few words:-

ESCAPED SERIAL KILLER

For a brief second she contemplated taking the long way, it was well lit, then decided against it. If she went up the back lane behind the shops she would get home much quicker.It's not like the murderer, whoever he or she was, would be here in the God forsaken Seahills. She grinned to herself as she entered the dark tree covered lane, but that's what she was, wasn't it...A murderer, here in the Seahills... And a very profitable one too.

Gary was number three and God was she pleased to get rid of this one, she shuddered, his habits were disgusting. To keep him sweet she'd let him perform the most perverted acts, the self same ones she'd endured as a child at the hands of her stepfather.

Did these perverts all do exactly the same?Is there a handbook on it some bloody where?

And the violence. Night after night of black market gore videos, he had more than one snuff video too. The creep.

She sighed, then her smile returned, he would get his comeuppance tonight alright, and the next one would be a helpless cripple in a wheel chair. No doubt about that.

The poison had been slowly doing its damage for over a month now, tonight would finish him off, so what if his friends got a little sick, that was all in the plan. She herself was a past master at acting sick, everyone would recover, the creep wouldn't though. No way.

A fine rain began to fall. Damn. Just had my hair done as well. She always had a cut and blow wave to celebrate, it had become a custom. She picked up speed her heels clacking on the pavement as she mentally ticked off a list to make sure she had everything she needed; the strongest curry powder available that would certainly cover any lingering bitterness the poison might leave, avocados for sweet to clean the palette. Nodding to herself, her smile grew wider.

No one could say she never gave her men a fucking good send off.

Too busy congratulating herself she failed to notice the figure detach itself from the large oak tree as she passed by; it was the unexpected sound of heavy footsteps behind her that caused her heart to go into overdrive. As the footsteps drew closer, so her heart beat faster.

A phrase she'd heard more than once surfaced from the jangled panicked thoughts in her head, 'those that live by the sword die by the sword.'

Was this it? What some would call poetic justice. A murderer to be murdered.

Unable to stop herself she looked over her right shoulder and got quite a shock to see a tall youth nearly abreast of her, in that one glance she took in the inked spider web covering half his face, the nose and eyebrow rings, the muscular set to his tall body and gasped as he stepped sideways bringing himself in front of her.

This was it she thought panicking, all that money hidden away and no one left to enjoy it, all her plans dead. She froze as he pulled something out of his pocket.

A knife? A gun?

'Have yer got a light Missus?' He asked holding a cigarette to his lips.

'Wha...no...go away.' She started to move, her heart pounding against her ribs. Asking for a light was just an excuse. Of course it was.

'Sorry...only asking.' He put the cigarette back in the box then transferred the packet from hand to pocket.

'Go away.' She started to hurry but he easily kept pace with her.

'I was gonna ask if you'd want me to walk to the end of the lane with yer like, only there's some street lights out further along, soon be real dark yer know Missus.'

She resisted the urge to tell him to fuck off, for all she knew he could be unstable and anything could set him off, he could also be the murderer.

'No thank you.'

'Suit yerself Missus, only trying to help, yer look a bit frightened, that's all.'

Who wouldn't be looking at that hideous tattoo. She thought but again kept quiet. She couldn't help but feel a bit foolish as he hurried off in front of her, he might be alright she thought, that's the problem these days you never can tell.

She took a step forward, staring at his retreating figure and failed to see the brick lying in the middle of the path. Suddenly she was down, her body sprawled across the path, her bag with the precious dinner surprises burst open and scattered every which way. Pain blazed white hot in her ankle.

'Please,' she pleaded as she sat up and rubbed it, 'don't be broken. Not tonight, please not tonight.'

She snorted, foolish to think God would even listen to her never mind help her. A vision of a hospital waiting room superimposed itself over that of her dinner guests sitting round her dining room table.

'Bastard,' then she jerked her head up as she heard a noise. Had he come back?

He was playing with her. He was the murderer after all.

She closed her eyes and shrank in on herself, the pain from her ankle momentarily forgotten as her body cringed waiting for the blow.

'Are you alright dear?' The voice had an Irish lilt to it.

She opened her eyes, it was full dark now and she had to strain to see, her night vision had never been much good. A man was coming towards her. Was that a dog collar he was wearing? Her heart lit up with hope. God hadn't deserted her at all in her hour of need, he'd sent a priest to help her.

'Betty. What the hell?' All pretence at an Irish accent disappeared as quickly as her sinking heart.

'Gary,' what was that fool doing out here dressed as a priest?

'I fell over that stupid brick...I thought, I thought you were a real bloody priest for a minute there.'

He bent to help her up, 'You've forgotten again haven't you, it's role play tonight, you know priests and tarts.'

She sighed, yes she had forgotten about the dress up part, seemed she was forgetting a lot these days. Fully upright she watched impatiently while he picked the strewn packages up.

'Do hurry up will you, this foot's bloody well killing me.'

'Last one dear.'

The last one, she was sure it was the parcel with the poison in, had managed to roll right to the end of the path.

'For God's sake,' she snapped, 'I can't stand up much longer.'

'I'm here now,' he took hold of her arm and placed it over his shoulder, 'it's not too far, if you lean on me do you think you can make it or shall I carry you?'

'No.' She almost shouted, her mind working over time.

What if he insists on making the curry, she could see her plans swiftly going down the drain, perhaps if she sent him on some errand she would be able to slip into the kitchen. She stopped for a moment and tested her foot then yanking it up yelped with the pain.

'Shit.'

'Don't fret dear, soon you won't feel the pain.'

'Huu.'

She'd been so busy thinking and fretting that she had not realised how close to the trees they were.

'Where are you going stupid, this isn't the way home.'

He sighed heavily.

'Well it's your home now dear.'

'Wha...' she got no further, his hands were round her throat, squeezing, squeezing, as she slid down the length of his body.

'Pity about the insurance money dear, it would have kept me going for a while but in this job you have to keep your wits about you...and never, never talk in your sleep.'

***

The owner of the newsagents shop carefully pinned the latest bulletin to the board.

TREBLE WIFE KILLER STILL ON RUN

Irish serial killer Gary Wilkinson spotted in the area...

Competition Time

Oh dear, we're at the end. You've read all the stories, mar-
velled at our interviewing skills and now you're wondering
just what you're going to do until the next issue of
Radgepacket hits the streets.

Well you might just be in luck because the mighty Ms
Quigley has, after some top level begging from our side, given
us some signed copies of her books 'Run for Home' and 'Bad
Moon Rising'...they're bloody good an all!

All you have to do to win a copy of a book is email :-

ed@bykerbooks.co.uk

with your address and the answer to this question.

**Sheila Quigley has written six crime novels set on
the fictional 'Seahills Estate' - what common theme
runs through the titles of all these novels?**

The closing date for this competition is 30th April 2009.

Please enter 'Radgepacket 2 Competition' as the subject line
of your email, all those that fail to do so disqualify themselves instantly.

Winners will be chosen at random and notified by email. The
editors decision is final and no correspondence will be
entered into if you don't win- so don't bother.

Right, what are you waiting for? Get cracking.

Printed in the United Kingdom
by Lightning Source UK Ltd.
136500UK00001B/97-99/P